THE ELEVENTH URBAN FARM FRESH ROMANCE

Joys of Juniper

VALERIE COMER

GreenWords Media

ACKNOWLEDGMENTS

Thank you for being a faithful reader of the Urban Farm Fresh Romance series! I appreciate you so much.

Thanks to Elizabeth Maddrey, first reader, idea-bouncer and excellent author in your own right. Thank you for providing sanity, humor, and kicks in the pants as needed!

Also thank you to Melanie D Snitker, author, friend, and beta reader. Your comments helped tighten and improve this story.

A big thank you to my fabulous editor, Nicole, who sees beyond words, punctuation, and sentence structure to the heart of the story.

I'm also grateful for the Christian Indie Authors Facebook group and my sister bloggers at Inspy Romance. These folks make a difference in my life every single day. I'm thrilled to walk beside them as we tell stories for Jesus!

Thank you to my Facebook friends, followers, street team, and reader group members for prayers, encouragement, and great fellowship.

Thanks to my husband, Jim, for research trips to

Spokane (although not during this coronavirus pandemic which has closed the Canada/USA border!) and talking through scenarios as needed — to say nothing of everyday love and support — and to my kids and grandgirls for cheering me on and embracing the idiosyncrasies of having an author for a mom and grandmother.

All my love and gratitude goes to Jesus, the One who invited me to experience His unending and passionate love and walks beside me every day. My prayer is that you see His love anew through the pages of this story.

Valerie Comer Bibliography

Urban Farm Fresh Romance

0. Promise of Peppermint (ebook only)
1. Secrets of Sunbeams
2. Butterflies on Breezes
3. Memories of Mist
4. Wishes on Wildflowers
5. Flavors of Forever
6. Raindrops on Radishes
7. Dancing at Daybreak
8. Glimpses of Gossamer
9. Lavished with Lavender
10. Cadence of Cranberries
11. Joys of Juniper

Christmas in Montana Romance

1. More Than a Tiara
2. Other Than a Halo
3. Better Than a Crown

Farm Fresh Romance

1. Raspberries and Vinegar
2. Wild Mint Tea
3. Sweetened with Honey
4. Dandelions for Dinner
5. Plum Upside Down
6. Berry on Top

Cavanagh Cowboys Romance
(Montana Ranches Christian Romance)

1. Marry Me for Real, Cowboy'
2. Give Me Another Chance, Cowboy
3. Let Me Off Easy, Cowboy

Saddle Springs Romance
(Montana Ranches Christian Romance)

1. The Cowboy's Christmas Reunion
2. The Cowboy's Mixed-Up Matchmaker
3. The Cowboy's Romantic Dreamer
4. The Cowboy's Convenient Marriage
5. The Cowboy's Belated Discovery
6. The Cowboy's Reluctant Bride

Garden Grown Romance
(Arcadia Valley Romance)

1. Sown in Love (ebook only)
2. Sprouts of Love
3. Rooted in Love
4. Harvest of Love

Riverbend Romance Novellas

1. Secretly Yours
2. Pinky Promise
3. Sweet Serenade
4. Team Bride
5. Merry Kisses

valeriecomer.com/books

*A*va Santoro should quit making friends with single women. Then she couldn't get roped into all these weddings, right? But maybe married women didn't make much better friends, since they were distracted by their husbands and, eventually, babies.

Not her, though, even if she wished it would happen. True love seemed to have found her unworthy. Her most recent boyfriend was now gaga over her cousin, and she'd been paired with today's groom's older brother. It couldn't get much worse. Basil was Ava's least favorite cousin, and she had plenty to pick from.

She'd smiled graciously for hours — or so it seemed — and the reception was just beginning. But now she was stuck between Basil and the bride, who was understandably busy making eyes at her brand-new husband.

"Almost over, huh?" Basil leaned a little closer. "You gonna be next? Got a significant other?"

She tried to edge away, but there was nowhere to go. "No boyfriend."

"You must be the only unhitched Santoro besides me. And the juveniles."

"Thanks for the reminder."

"It's not so bad. Give it long enough, and they quit having expectations. Then you can do whatever you want."

"Like you *ever* cared," she muttered under her breath.

Of course, he heard her and responded with a low chuckle. "Oh, I cared once upon a time. But you make one little mistake, become the family black sheep, and — poof — it's suddenly sort of freeing."

That's how it looked to him? He was full of himself. "You were drunk. You ran a police checkpoint and went to jail. That's what you call freedom?"

Basil uttered a sardonic laugh. "You have no idea."

"You're right." Ava grabbed her clutch and pushed out her chair. "Now, please excuse me. I need to use the restroom."

"See what I mean about being a pariah?"

She almost pivoted and told him exactly why she was shunning him. It had little to do with his teensy-tiny *mistake* and everything to do with his derisive attitude. How could he live with himself?

Ava strode to the restroom in the Bridgeview Community Center, dodging past the servers preparing to bring plates out to the tables. For a fleeting moment, she wished she were one of them. She worked part-time at the bistro in charge of tonight's catering and had served at plenty of special events like this one. Wouldn't it have been nice to get a paycheck for smiling and nodding to hundreds of people instead of being stuck with Basil? If only she could have said no to Marley, but a girl just didn't do that to a friend. The temptation had been mighty strong once she found out Alex had asked his older brother to be best man.

She couldn't stay in the restroom long enough to get her temper completely under control. That would take a week of sub-zero weather, but maybe she could survive another hour before disappearing again.

Eating ought to take up some of Basil's attention. He'd probably complain how it wasn't up to the standards of the award-winning Seattle restaurant where he worked. Imagine a college grad his age, waiting tables. Yeah, Basil was just as much a loser as she remembered, not that they really knew each other. With their six-year age difference, they hadn't exactly chummed around as kids.

Ava tested out her glamor smile in the mirror. She'd been in the performing arts since she was three. She could do this. She sashayed out of the restroom.

And nearly bowled over a blond server with a platter of plates. Instinctively, she managed to avoid a collision by rising to her tiptoes with her hands high and her gut sucked in. Dance moves to the rescue. "Sorry!"

"You okay?" He asked politely enough, but Ava could sense he knew it was all her fault, because it was.

"Sure. And good job keeping that thing balanced. I'm impressed."

He rolled his eyes as Hailey, one of the bistro owners, turned to relieve him of two more loaded plates.

Ava frowned a little before remembering the stage smile she'd donned. Where had Hailey found this surly guy? Ava had worked at Bridgeview Bakery and Bistro on and off since high school, fitting shifts around classes and dance recitals and substitute teaching, but she'd never seen him before. She'd definitely have remembered.

Looked like the head table had already been served. Ava slid back into her chair and lifted her fork.

"Who's that guy with Hailey?"

And... there was Basil nattering on again as though Ava were his sole source of local information and entertainment. Maybe she was.

Ava glanced over, taking a closer look at Hailey. When had her boss worn this much makeup or fixed her hair so formally? Hailey had catered plenty of weddings — Ava had helped with her fair share of them — and this was a first. And that little black dress clung to her curves.

Who was she trying to impress? Server Boy? That didn't seem right, although Hailey tended to chase anyone with a Y chromosome, and the guy was reasonably good-looking. Yellowy blond hair, strong jaw... plus it seemed there might be a muscle or two rippling beneath his white shirt.

"Ava?"

"I don't know him. Is the entree good?"

Basil shrugged. "Okay, I guess. It's food." He scowled as he glanced back at Hailey and the guy working with her.

Wait. What? Basil and Hailey were two of a kind, flirting with anyone who'd look twice, both flitting around like butterflies — wouldn't Basil love that comparison? — never sticking with one flower for long. Could they...?

Nah. Imagining unrequited love between that unlikely pair was a sure sign there were too many starry-eyed lovers in Ava's life these days.

Still watching, she reached for her wine glass. Crash! Over it went, sending a widening burgundy puddle toward the edge of the table. Toward her peach-colored dress.

Way to be a klutz, Ava.

She skidded her chair back to get away as Basil surged to his feet, throwing all the linen napkins he could grasp onto the spill. "Hey, can we get some help over here?" he hollered.

Heat suffused Ava's cheeks. Oh, man, way to draw all eyes to herself and now Basil.

Server Boy set the platter down, grabbed several towels, and jogged over. He caught the edge of the burgundy lake before it turned into a waterfall. In another minute, he and Hailey had rolled away the offending tablecloth while the wedding party lifted their plates and glasses. A few seconds later, a fresh cloth covered the table, the plates were set down, and the meal resumed as though nothing had happened.

Except for Ava. She took a couple of small bites, but it seemed her stomach would reject even that, so she crossed her utensils on her plate.

"Not going to eat your dinner?" Basil eyed her portion.

Seriously? "Be my guest."

"If you insist." He swapped their plates.

Ava couldn't watch. The noise in the community center had resumed its previous level once the drama at the head table was over. She located her parents chatting with some of Dad's brothers and their wives then found her younger sister surrounded by several of their cousins. Her gaze lingered on dozens of neighbors and friends and church members. She loved Bridgeview.

Except that everyone had witnessed her humiliation. Graceful, poised Ava Santoro, dance and music teacher, tipping over a wine glass like a butterfingered kid after nearly running over that cute server.

Not that she'd ever have a chance with a guy like that.

She didn't want one. Especially not if he was interested in a woman like Hailey North.

It was an uncharitable thought. Ava loved the camaraderie at the bistro, both among the staff and with the regulars. The place exuded a joyous atmosphere, and that had as much to do with Hailey as with her co-owner, Kass Ferguson.

Ava simply preferred Boss Hailey to Manhunter Hailey, and tonight the woman was fluttering her eyelashes at Server Boy like he was Adonis. Ava should warn him, but then, he looked like a grownup, and if he was lapping up all this attention, Hailey was his problem.

Good luck with her, Server Boy.

SETH DONAHUE LINED up with the other waitstaff, watching for the opportunity to remove the remaining plates. He couldn't help glancing over at the head table where the dark-haired beauty sat between the bride and the best man, who gobbled from her plate.

She seemed to have regained her poise, but she hadn't eaten more than two or three bites. One of those women who watched her waistline so avidly that she was starving herself to death? He knew enough women with eating disorders, and she didn't really carry the signs.

"Thanks, Seth. You're doing great." His boss for the evening leaned closer and rested her fingertips on his arm.

Did she have no sense of propriety? He barely knew her and had done his best not to give off easy vibes. He knew far too well what those looked like. After too many years living the other life, he was done.

He scratched his shoulder, effectively dislodging her hand. "Thanks. What's next?"

"A few speeches. Cutting of the cake." She pointed to the towering multi-colored confection on a side table. "Serving dessert. Clearing dishes and cleaning the kitchen while they start dancing."

The maid of honor was going to dance with the best man. Great. But Seth didn't have to watch. A quick glance at his boss revealed she was contemplating the same couple he was. That was weird. "Who is that?"

Hailey straightened and looked away. "Just the groom's brother."

Like he was eyeing the dude. "I meant the girl."

"Oh." Twin pink dots rose high on Hailey's cheeks. "The groom's cousin and best friend of the bride."

Which made her the best man's cousin, too. Seth had no right to feel the relief sliding down his spine.

"Marley works at the bistro, and so does Ava and one of the other bridesmaids. It's why I needed to hire extras for tonight."

Marley was the bride, which meant... "The maid of honor's name is Ava?"

"Ava Santoro." Her fingertips fluttered against his sleeve again. "Schmooze on your own time."

Seth's eyebrows shot up. "Like you're doing?" Uh... he should have bit back those words. She was his boss for the evening.

Hailey snatched her hand away. "Looks like the far table is ready for clearing."

"I'll get their plates right now." He didn't even look to see who else was bussing over there. Probably not Hailey, since it was surrounded by folks middle-aged and up with nary a single guy in sight. Okay, maybe he wasn't being fair to her. Maybe she was just a touchy-feely person, but all that attention made him uncomfortable. It made him feel he'd been hired mostly as a prop. Wasn't that a laugh? Seth Donahue wasn't the kind of guy who attracted women like Hailey North, thank the Lord.

And where that thought had once been a glib reminder of his churchy upbringing, these days, he meant it. He'd had his Prodigal Son moment, thankfully before his dad and stepmom's accident, since he now had custody of his two half-sisters. What did a guy of twenty-eight who'd wasted most of a decade know about preteen girls? But at least he'd been able to step in before Beatrice and Peyton were sent into foster care.

Which made him super attractive to women. Not. Who wanted to date a guy with two kids who just might be young enough to be his offspring? The girls were with a sitter tonight, someone arranged by Hailey. She'd been fairly desperate to have him serve this event. Why? None of his business. He had work to do. Honest work he'd be paid for.

An hour later, he was done with his cleanup assignments and stood in the kitchen doorway, watching as the wedding party danced. The best man and maid of honor swung closer, more gracefully than he'd have expected from someone as bumbling as she seemed to be.

Both of their gazes fastened on him in the same instant. The best man's cool and calculating. The maid of honor's desperate.

Seth took a step forward. Damsels in distress were his specialty. Then he stopped, because he was only waitstaff tonight, and she likely didn't mean to signal for his attention the way it appeared.

And then Ava twirled elegantly out of the guy's arms and straight into Seth's like she did know what she was doing. "Dance with me? Please?"

"But..."

The best man glowered at him. But no, his gaze roved past Seth to Hailey, who pivoted away, her color heightened. Interesting. But that still left Seth with a raven-haired stunner in his arms who smelled of gardenias and looked up at him with pretty blue eyes.

Hailey'd never said he couldn't dance — why would she have thought he'd be tempted? — and he was off the clock. Why not just go for it? One dance, a little extra bonus for his evening's work?

He rested a palm on the woman's waist, clasped her hand with his, and twirled her back into the melee. "I don't believe we've been introduced. I'm Seth Donahue, and you are...?"

2

---

*T*he guy was smooth.

He spun Ava out and then back in as effortlessly as most of the guys she'd danced with professionally, and she couldn't help her smile of appreciation.

"You're a good dancer." Seth twirled her.

Ava laughed. "I ought to be. I've been dancing since I was three. Probably younger."

"Oh, yeah? That explains it."

"You're pretty good, yourself."

"I ought to be." He waggled his eyebrows. "I've been tripping over my own two feet even longer than you've been dancing."

She couldn't help the peal of laughter that came from his words. "I did my share of clumsy tonight, that's for sure. Sorry about nearly running you over earlier."

"My natural grace and balance saved the world from eight plates of prime rib, mashed potatoes, and gravy dumped all over the floor."

"To say nothing of broccoli. At least there weren't any beets."

He raised his brows at her. Waited.

"The spatters would have looked like blood."

Seth snickered and twirled her out.

Ava couldn't remember when she'd had this much fun. No one was watching her form or judging her. Well, her grandmother might be, but that was Nonna's problem, not hers.

"Have you been working for Hailey long?"

He pulled her in a little faster than she expected, right into his arms, as his smile froze in place.

She stared up at him, breathlessly, for just a second or two before she responded to the music again. What had that been all about?

"I answered an ad in the Spokesman Review last week. You know her?"

"I've worked at the bistro on and off since I was in high school. So, yeah, I know her pretty well."

"Interesting." He didn't look interested. "Tell me about yourself."

"There's not much to say," she hedged.

Seth's warm hands shifted slightly, not enough to be indecent, just enough to remind her of their intimate closeness.

"I'm a teacher. Music and dance at some of the nearby elementary schools. A day each at three of them, hoping to add two more for the new school year, but I haven't heard back yet."

"Impressive." He offered a sideways smile.

She was twenty-six. Her feats would be far more impressive if she were five years younger. "And you?"

He looked past her. "Between situations right now, but looking for something permanent."

Seth seemed about to say more, but the music stopped, and she released her hold on him as he did the same. They stood for a second, staring at each other.

The world ground to a standstill. The community center fizzled and faded, taking the bride, the groom, and the two hundred wedding guests with it. All that remained was her and Seth and the — something — that zinged between them.

From another realm, the slow measures of Anne Murray's classic filtered into her awareness, and she took a step closer, right into his waiting arms.

"Could I have this dance?" he asked softly, echoing the title.

"You may." *For the rest of my life.* Which was ridiculous, since they'd only just met.

This was no energetic swing but a fully romantic couple's dance. Ava ignored the thought as she nestled into Seth's strong arms, her cheek resting on his chest. As one, they swayed smoothly to the rhythm.

Was this what Cinderella had felt like when she danced with Prince Charming? Was the clock going to strike midnight and turn Ava Santoro into an ordinary teacher in ballet flats once again?

Probably. She'd never seen Seth before tonight, and she'd likely never see him again... though if he asked for her phone number, she'd hand it over without a blink. But it wasn't likely. He didn't even have a job, so he wouldn't be looking to start something with anyone, let alone her.

Did she know of any job openings? She didn't have a clue what degree he might have or his job experience or life goals. It was impossible to make suggestions at this stage.

She felt his cheek rest on the side of her head. His nose was probably stuck in her bun, and that elicited a tiny giggle.

Seth's hands tightened on her back. "What's so funny?" he growled in her ear.

"Nothing," she whispered back, angling just enough to look at him. He was so close she could kiss him.

What on earth was she thinking? Ava pulled back a little further, reducing the temptation. She might have been ignoring the fact that two hundred family members and neighborhood friends surrounded them, but it was time to remember. She wasn't going to give them all stories to tell for decades to come.

Remember Alex and Marley's wedding, when cousin Ava danced with one of the servers all night and then kissed him? Don't be like her.

To say nothing of Nonna's tirade. It would contain a reminder her younger sister had been swept away by a smooth talker in high school. Now twenty-year-old Dafne was raising her son by herself.

Yeah. Don't be like Daf.

Ava froze for a second and missed her step, nearly stomping on Seth's foot. "Sorry."

His eyes flitted to her lips then back up.

She was in trouble if he was having the same thoughts she was. All she knew was the guy's name, that he didn't have a job, and could move well enough to make her forget herself.

"I should probably dance with someone else," she blurted out.

His eyes narrowed a little as he steered her out of the throng. "Sorry if I took advantage of you. I'm just a server."

"No, it's not your fault. And besides, I practically begged you to rescue me from my cousin."

"You did." He quirked a lopsided grin that didn't reach his eyes. "But it wasn't my place to keep things going."

"I enjoyed it." Probably a little too much.

They stood beside the Tesla Power Wall that had powered the entire community center for going on five years now. Ava reached out and pressed her palm against the white surface as though it could give her personal strength.

"I did, too." Seth rubbed the back of his neck. "It was nice meeting you, Ava Santoro."

"Same to you, Seth Donahue."

This was when he'd ask for her contact information. Right? But he bit his lip as his gaze roved her face. She was doing the same, memorizing his features to remember always.

Seth gave her another awkward grin and a nod before he turned and strode into the kitchen nearby. A moment later she heard the back door open and close.

He was gone. He hadn't asked for her number.

She braced herself against the wall and closed her eyes.

"Who was that?" her sister asked quietly.

Ava took a deep breath and eyed Dafne. "Just a guy Hailey hired to serve tonight."

Dafne's eyebrows rose. "*Just a guy*? Looked like you thought more than that."

"For a few minutes, yes." Ava smoothed her dress. "Enjoying the reception?"

Her sister shrugged. "If you call dancing with Dad and

the uncles and Peter fun, sure. You know how protective our big brother can be."

This was not the moment to see if she could spot Peter and his bride of six months. If she made eye contact, he'd be over here in a flash. Best to avoid that and stay focused on Dafne. "You should dance with someone else."

"Ava, quit trying to set me up. You know my life isn't the same as yours."

"Just because you have a toddler doesn't mean you can't find love. Steer clear of Connor Hamelin, though."

"He's not here. And besides, I learned my lesson with him. What decent guy would take on a girl like me with a kid? No one, that's who, but I'll be fine."

"Gavin's lucky to have you for a mom."

Dafne reached out and gave Ava a hug. "And he's lucky to have you for an aunt. If you need some recovery time after all that dancing with the server, come on, and let's get some of Aunt Winnie's biscotti."

༄

THE GIRLS WERE STILL UP when Seth paid the sitter and sent her off in an Uber.

"I thought I told you girls to be good for Jenny."

"We were," eight-year-old Peyton announced.

"Then you should be sound asleep. It's ten-thirty."

"She asked if we wanted to go to bed, and we said no, we didn't." Peyton sounded so reasonable. The teen sitter wasn't likely up to the pair of them.

Seth raised his eyebrows at Beatrice. "You knew what she meant. Both of you."

Beatrice shrugged. "Loosen up."

Only ten, but the attitude of a teen already showed. Not for the first time, panic swelled up in Seth's chest. How on earth was he going to raise two girls into responsible adults? He'd certainly not been the kind of teen or young adult he wanted the girls to emulate. "No backtalk," he reminded her.

"You're not my dad."

"I know, Beatrice. I know. Everything is rough, but we're going to make it. We just need to stick together."

Nothing warm shone from her eyes. Peyton, on the other hand, wrapped her arms around his waist. "I'm sorry, Seth."

"It's okay, Pey. But it's definitely bedtime. How about you girls get your pajamas on? Have you had a snack?" One thing he'd learned was that these two could never fall asleep with empty stomachs.

"Could we have popcorn?" wheedled Peyton, looking up at him.

What was another half hour? "Sure. I'll get it started. Come on out when you're changed." Seth waited until Beatrice gave a reluctant nod before he exited their room and headed into the kitchen.

Oh, God, how was he going to get through this? Seth'd had no right to dream for that little bit of time tonight. He'd had no right to gaze into Ava Santoro's beautiful blue eyes and entertain kissing her for even one second. He'd danced into a fairytale, and it had taken every bit of his self-control to stumble back out of it. A beautiful woman. A teacher. A Santoro at a Santoro wedding. Hailey had told him just enough to know that while the family wasn't crazy wealthy, they were certainly comfortably situated.

Not Seth. His dad and stepmom's accident a month ago

had only been the first thing. He'd had to list their house to pay the contractor who'd been in the middle of remodeling. Thankfully there would be funds left over from the quick sale, enough for a damage deposit and a few months' rent while Seth tried to put things together.

He didn't want to spend a penny of it on himself, but the girls' future was tied to his, and they needed food and shelter now if they were to survive to adulthood. He needed a job, and fast.

They'd probably be better off in foster care than with their loser big brother. Would their Aunt Eliza and Uncle John be a better choice?

He'd had this battle within his head so many times in the past few weeks. If only he hadn't misspent his youth. A guy his age could be in much better shape to care for his siblings if he hadn't worked just enough for booze and parties.

I have redeemed you.

Seth closed his eyes as the kernels began to pop. Only the faith he'd reclaimed a year and a half ago kept him going now.

"Was it a pretty wedding?" Peyton asked wistfully.

He tugged her to his side for a quick hug. "Yes, it was." His mind slid to Ava.

"Was it all pink and lace and flowers?"

"One of the bridesmaids wore pink. The maid of honor's dress was light orange—"

"That's called peach." Beatrice rolled her eyes.

"Okay, peach. And the other two wore blue and green."

"Four bridesmaids," Peyton said dreamily. "Was there a flower girl sprinkling rose petals?"

"I don't know. I didn't go to the wedding, just the reception. I wasn't a guest, just a server."

"How about a ring bearer?" His sister sounded like she realized he wouldn't know the answer but couldn't help asking anyway.

Seth shrugged. "Beatrice, want to melt some butter?"

She made a face but scooped a large blob into a pot.

"Less than that." Feeding these kids was costly enough without going through butter like it was water. If only...

He'd spent half an hour this evening dreaming about life in an alternate dimension. What if he hadn't been the prodigal son and wasted a decade of his life with nothing to show for it? What if his sisters' parents hadn't died? What if Dad and Lori hadn't stretched their finances right to the breaking point, rendering their daughters nearly destitute, homeless, and dependent on Seth?

If all those things had played out differently, especially Seth's youthful choices, this evening would have been different, too.

He'd have asked for Ava Santoro's phone number, for sure.

He might even have been brave enough to kiss her, which would have been all kinds of stupid since it wasn't even their first date.

There'd never be a first date, because all those what-ifs hadn't happened. She had it all together. She'd never date a guy like him.

She definitely shouldn't.

3

*A*va wandered into her favorite refuge, the permaculture garden Wade and Rebekah had created from a vacant lot along the riverside. A hedge of juniper lined the street, while fruit and nut trees defined the edge along the park next door. Brambles shielded the area from the river and left a corner for beehives that Ava's cousin Jasmine tended. A few chickens scrabbled around the perennial herbs near the burgeoning rhubarb.

Her own dad and uncles had bought the lot and donated it to the community for this purpose, just one of several foodie ventures in the neighborhood. The community garden beside Nonna's house was great, too, providing a place where residents could grow some vegetables and enjoy the communal herbs and flowers. There was even a fountain and a picnic table.

Ava preferred the wilder food forest. It called to her, somehow. It might have been the proximity to the river. She rounded a particularly large bush and gasped. "Sorry, I didn't see you here!"

Wade Roper pushed his Fish and Wildlife baseball cap further up his forehead. "Ava! You know you're always welcome. It's not private property."

"I know, but..."

He waved a hand. "No buts. Had you heard we finally got a grant to create a wet area for mint and other plants that like wet feet? The agricultural department is donating some experimental apple varieties, too."

"Oh, that's fabulous!"

"We received enough to employ someone for a couple of months. I wish I could do it all myself, but I'm spread too thin as it is."

"I could help out." Even as Ava said the words, she knew she didn't have the skills to implement the plan.

"Aren't you busy?" Wade leaned on his shovel.

"School's out next week. But yeah, I do have dance classes scheduled throughout the summer. Plus Kass has me on the schedule at the bistro." Kass was Hailey's cousin, and the two of them ran the business together. Hailey was in charge of the kitchen, and Kass managed the front.

"That's what I thought." Wade grinned. "I'm thankful for your heart for the project, though. Too bad Peter and Jasmine have most of the neighborhood's teen boys working for Bridgeview Backyards. I'll have to look farther afield."

"Is it the kind of grant that requires someone to be in school?"

Wade shook his head. "No, it's discretionary on my part whom to hire. Know anyone?"

Ava thought of Seth, but he was looking for something permanent, and this was only for the summer. Besides, she didn't have his contact information.

Hailey did. But there was no way on the planet Ava was

going to ask her for it. That would lead to more personal questions and discussions than Ava cared to have with her boss. No doubt Hailey would already have something to say about the dancing.

Seth was on his own. She needed to get over how she'd felt in his arms, listening to his heartbeat during that last slow dance.

"Well, I've been praying about it since I heard yesterday. I'm sure God will send just the right person along soon."

Ava eyed him. "How do you have that kind of faith? And patience, too?"

Wade chuckled. "Lots of experience knowing that God will never let me down. Learned that in a big way when He brought Rebekah back into my life seven years ago, and He's been reinforcing the lesson ever since."

"You guys are so great together that it's hard to believe you ever had a hiccup in your relationship."

"It wasn't a hiccup." Wade took off his cap, ran his fingers through his hair, and replaced it. "I didn't hear from her for over four years. I never dreamed God would work a miracle to bring us back together."

"That's probably what makes Rebekah such a good counselor for the kids at Bridgeview Elementary."

"I'm sure it is. She definitely had some rough spots in her life."

Ava had heard Rebekah's testimony several times, so she just nodded. "I'll keep an ear out for someone who could use a summer job, but honestly, I don't mind volunteering some. Just point me at a job that needs doing. Maintenance or something."

Wade glanced around his domain, satisfaction evident on his face. "The beauty of permaculture is that there isn't a ton that needs doing on a regular basis. But the space is underutilized, so if you want to pick rhubarb or keep the comfrey cut back, that would be great. If you can make use of the berries as they ripen, go for it, or donate them to someone else. I know Tony wishes we had enough to supply the restaurant, but there simply isn't that kind of volume. I think he's planted some raspberries behind Antonio's."

One of Ava's cousins, Tony had opened his own restaurant just down the street about a year ago. Another one of the Santoro uncles' investment projects, to say nothing of all the vision and labor they'd contributed to renovating the older building into an Italian villa.

Ava didn't eat there much. The place was perfect for date night, and not so perfect for a single woman on a part-time teacher's salary. Besides, she could cook, too. She just didn't quite have Tony's imagination to tweak Nonna's recipes they'd all grown up with.

Didn't matter. She loved tradition. Didn't she? Then why did everything in Bridgeview seem to stifle her?

꩜

BEATRICE CROSSED her arms and looked around the small apartment. "I don't want to live here."

Seth didn't want to, either, though it was way nicer than most of the places he'd stayed in during his delinquent years.

"I like the wood floors," put in Peyton. "And there's a nice view of the river. Can we go down there sometimes and have a picnic?"

Beatrice rolled her eyes.

"Sure. I don't see why not. Beatrice, which bedroom

would you like for you and your sister to share? I'll take the other one."

She pointed immediately to the larger one at the back of the apartment — the one with two windows.

Fine, he'd take the smaller space with the view of the building next door. It wasn't like he had time to sit and gaze off into daydreams, anyway. "Beatrice, we're here partly because the school is only a few blocks away, and it's a really good one. They even have a gardening program all the grades participate in."

"Great. We'll come home covered in dirt."

"Water cures that."

"Whatever."

Just exactly how much backtalk should he let the ten-year-old get away with? Man, he needed someone to talk to. Someone who knew about kids and grief and change and what was normal and what was not.

"Okay, well, we'll get stuff moved this afternoon. Dan Ranta said he could bring his truck by and maybe a friend or two to help haul the heavy stuff." Bless the guy for accepting Seth as a friend, even though Seth had made some moves on Dixie back when she and Dan were split up. He'd been on a break from Diana, but they'd got together again briefly before he'd returned to his childhood faith and left her behind forever.

"I don't want to move out of our house." Peyton's eyes filled with tears. "How will Mom and Dad know where to find us if they come back?"

"They're not coming back, stupid. They're *dead*."

Peyton cringed away from her sister, and the tears spilled over.

Seth wrapped an arm around the younger girl. "Beatrice

is right. They're not coming back, but I know it's hard for both of you. I get it."

"You don't get anything." Beatrice scowled at him.

"Hey, kiddo. I understand a whole lot more than you think I do." He kept his tone easy and his smile gentle. Didn't look like he convinced her, though.

An hour later, they were back at the house. Dan and a friend he introduced as Wade began loading the heavy furniture into two pickup trucks.

"Dixie's excited you're going to be living nearby." Dan looked between the girls. "And Mandy wants to be friends with your sisters."

They'd need friends, for sure. Seth hated that he was pulling them away from absolutely everything they'd ever known.

"How old is Mandy?" Peyton wanted to know.

"She's seven, just finishing first grade."

"She's just a *child*," sniffed Beatrice.

"No one said she wasn't." Seth pulled Beatrice close around her shoulders, but she twisted away.

"I'll be her friend." Peyton eyed her sister then Seth.

"Sounds good." Dan grinned. "We'll have you guys over soon."

Peyton beamed. "Okay."

Seth helped carry furniture out to the trucks then gave Dan the apartment key. With both girls underfoot, he might as well stay at the house and stage the boxes for the next trip. It would be nice to have a place to send the girls today, but he couldn't afford a sitter, and they were old enough to stay out of the way. If only Beatrice wasn't so determined to see the worst in everything.

He immediately chastised himself for those uncharitable

thoughts. He wasn't a ten-year-old who'd just lost her parents. He'd left home when his dad's new wife, Lori, had announced her pregnancy with Beatrice. He just hadn't been able to stomach the thought of his father starting over again with a new family when his attention had always been focused on his son.

Yeah, regrets. Seth had them by the boatload, but dwelling on them changed nothing. God had forgiven him. Seth just needed to keep remembering that.

By the end of the afternoon, the house sat empty except for a few loads for the dump, and Dan and Wade had set up the bunkbed in the girls' new room. Beatrice was in there with the door closed, and Seth could only hope she was unpacking her clothes into the spacious closet.

The apartment was in a building with twelve units, four on each floor. He'd scored a spot on the main level, which meant neighbor noise above and below, but it couldn't be helped. The location was good, close to a playground and basketball court under the bridge, a community church, and the elementary school he'd told his sisters about. That it was also near to the community center where he'd danced with Ava for a blissful half hour was not something he'd report to the girls.

Maybe he'd see her around the neighborhood at times. He kind of hoped not, because then she'd fully recognize the loser he was. A guy his age with two kids, no degree, and no job. Yeah. She'd definitely steer clear of him then. He'd save her the bother by evasion if he saw her.

Wade stuck out his hand. "Sure nice to meet you, Seth. My wife and I live just a few blocks away, right by the river. I'd like to invite you to Bridgeview Bible Church if you're interested. Quite a few of your neighbors attend there, and

I think you'll find Pastor Tomas Ramirez to be engaging and insightful."

"I noticed the church nearby," Seth admitted. "Hopefully, we'll check it out." If he could get the girls out the door on a Sunday morning.

"Anything else you need to get settled into Bridgeview?"

Seth laughed. "Just a job. But wait." He held up a cautionary finger. "Not just any job. Either one that pays well enough for childcare, or one where I can bring the girls along. So maybe what I'm really asking for is a miracle."

Wade eyed him thoughtfully. "A miracle, huh? God is in the business of those, you know."

"I know. I've asked. I just haven't seen one drop into my lap lately."

"Any experience with digging or pumps or landscaping?"

"I haven't worked for Dan's landscaping company, if that's what you're asking."

"Sorry." Dan shook his head. "If I had more contracts, I'd bring you on for sure."

Wade chuckled as he looked between them. "Similar skillset, I'm sure."

"Digging and planting, sure. Pumps... not so much, but I can read a manual and figure most anything out." Seth grinned. "There's a how-to video on YouTube for everything." No point in mentioning that he had three-quarters of a degree in engineering.

"I've got a grant to hire someone for ten weeks down at the food forest by the river, doing all those things. Short term, but it would buy you time to look for something more permanent."

Seth stared at the man he'd just met. "Seriously?"

"Yeah. The grant came through a couple of days ago for

the full amount we applied for. I wasn't counting on that. I've been asking God to show me who He's got for the project. Might that be you?"

"The girls..." Seth gestured toward Peyton, who stood on a chair putting plates in a cupboard.

"It doesn't bother me if they hang around with you while you work. It may not be ideal for them, but they'd get lots of fresh air, anyway. My wife is a counselor at the elementary school, so she'll be off for the summer soon, home with our kids right next door."

"And we're just half a block away," put in Dan. "I work all day, but Dixie's usually around. She serves two or three evenings a week over at Antonio's, that new Italian restaurant toward downtown."

"I... you don't know me. Don't know my abilities or anything."

Wade shrugged. "A friend of Dan and Dixie's is a friend of mine. That's the Bridgeview way. We look out for each other around here."

Dan snapped his fingers. "That reminds me. Dixie said to ask what the girls' favorite pizza is. We're ordering delivery for you tonight. It's been a long day for you, and I know your kitchen isn't put together. Though your helper is working hard at it."

Seth glanced at Peyton. "She's a great helper. And I want to say we don't need help, but... thank you. We accept."

"Yay!" Peyton beamed. "Cheese pizza is the best."

While Seth loved his loaded with five kinds of meat and sausage. "Cheese sounds fine."

"You sure, man? They'll do half and half. Or, wait, never mind. I'll order two. Then you've got leftovers for tomorrow."

"Dan..."

The other guy held up his hand. "You already accepted."

"I don't know what to say."

"Thanks is enough." Dan grinned.

"Come on down to the food forest tomorrow evening sometime? I'll show you around, and you can see what you think of the project." Wade dug into his wallet and handed over a business card. "Just give me a call to make sure I'm around, but I should be."

The two men shook hands with Seth and went into the corridor. He moved to the doorway to watch them head down the stairs, but he couldn't see around the landing to the building's exit.

"Hey, I think God answered my prayer," he heard Wade say from down below.

"Oh, really? I've been praying, too," a woman's voice answered.

Seth grasped the doorframe. He knew that voice. It belonged to the woman he couldn't get out of his mind.

4

*A*va climbed the stairs to the third-floor apartment she shared with her cousin just in time to hear the door click shut on the apartment directly below theirs. It had been empty for a couple of weeks, so new neighbors must have moved in. She and Brittany should bring down a batch of cookies or something.

She opened her own door. "Britt?" And then her gaze landed on her cousin making out with Ava's former boyfriend in the living room beyond. They'd split up a couple of months ago, and she knew he'd moved on to dating Brittany, but seriously? The very same sofa where she'd snuggled close on movie nights was Duncan's platform for kissing her cousin with more passion than Ava thought he possessed? To say nothing of roving hands. Whoa.

Ava closed her eyes, but she couldn't unsee the vision in front of her.

A scrambling sound came from the living room. "Ava! You're home early."

"I'm actually ten minutes late." She turned to set her

briefcase in the closet. With any luck, by the time she turned around they'd be three feet apart and not quite so flushed. For good measure, she counted to twenty before entering the small open kitchen beside the entry. Only after she'd poured herself a glass of iced tea from the fridge did she dare allow her gaze to lift over the peninsula into the living room.

Duncan stood looking out the expansive window as he adjusted the collar of his shirt. Brittany walked toward the peninsula, her long dark hair disheveled and her gaze guilty.

Ava raised her eyebrows but managed to keep her mouth zipped.

"Duncan was just leaving."

"Good." What was the appropriate response to the guy Ava had dated for six months? It certainly wasn't anything like *nice to see you again* or *fancy meeting you here*. More like *get out and don't come back*. Didn't Duncan have the sense God gave little gummy worms to know that it was more than just bad form to be caught in a semi-compromising position in his ex-girlfriend's own home?

"Nice to see you again, Ava." Duncan offered an awkward smile as he came up beside Brittany. He patted her shoulder then strolled out the door.

As soon as it clicked shut behind him, Ava slammed her fist against the countertop. "What on earth were you thinking?"

"It's not like you think."

"Maybe it depends on what I'm thinking."

"We didn't... we haven't gone all the way."

Ava drained her tall glass as she fought for control of her words. "Saving that for the weekend?"

"Ava! I can't believe you said that."

"I can't believe where I saw his hands."

Brittany looked down as she traced the pattern of the old Formica countertop with a fingertip. "I told him to stop."

"Before or after he unbuttoned your top?"

"You're probably just jealous."

Ava felt her eyes bulge. "Are you freaking kidding me? I broke up with him, not the other way around. You know that. I broke up with him for like a hundred reasons, and only one of them had anything to do with his traveling hands. He's an insensitive jerk."

"You're wrong about him. He's amazing."

She'd once thought so, too, but *that* was the part she'd been wrong about. "Just don't wind up pregnant like Dafne did."

"Your little sister was sixteen years old and dating Connor Hamelin behind your parents' backs. What did she think would happen?"

"Listen to yourself, Brittany Jane Santoro. It had nothing to do with her age and everything to do with her actions. Do you think she didn't care if she got pregnant or not? That she made a rational decision to have sex with him without regard for any possible consequences? It's not just a matter of protected sex, Britt. You give your virginity to Duncan, and you'll never get it back. That's what Daf regrets. She doesn't regret Gavin. Sure, being twenty and in college while parenting a toddler is tough, but her son is not her regret."

"You done preaching?"

"Britt."

"Sorry." Brittany sighed. "It will be okay, Ava. Thank you

for your concern. I know it's my night to make supper, but... ah... I haven't started. I'll fix a salad, okay?"

"Sure." Ava retreated to her bedroom and changed into a pair of jean shorts and a pink tank top. How much should she push her cousin? Did Aunt Winnie have any idea what was going on? Ava doubted it. Brittany's mom had married Charlie Jalonen only a couple of months ago, and she didn't look like she had braincells for anyone but her new husband. Probably as it should be, but still. And if she *could* think of something else, it was Britt's brother Dominic's wedding in a couple of weeks. He was marrying Charlie's daughter Katri.

Blergh. Another wedding Ava couldn't get out of, but at least she wasn't in the wedding party this time. Maybe Hailey would let her work the reception.

And that brought her mind around to Server Boy. No, he had a name. A gorgeous, strong name. Seth Donahue.

Ava disassembled her bun to shed the last of her teacher persona and began to brush out her long hair. Seth seemed to have liked her hair up, though, as they danced.

Didn't matter. Her reaction to Brittany had at least as much to do with rejection as with protection. It wasn't just Duncan. There'd been too many boyfriends who pushed the boundaries and found themselves in her ex column. Why couldn't Ava attract the right kind of guy? Seth wasn't that kind, either. She seriously needed a... a minister, or something. A man as pure as the driven snow. Someone who'd appreciate her.

She met her own gaze in the mirror. Seriously. She wasn't jealous of Brittany, was she?

Maybe a little bit. Not of snagging Duncan. But of being so fun and optimistic. Yeah, Britt was likely to land in a heap of trouble if she didn't make better choices, but at least she was enjoying her twenties. She had a great, steady job in graphic design that offered an outlet for her creativity.

And here was Ava, trying to teach twelve-year-old boys how to dance without permanently crippling the girls in their class. Trying to teach kids to play the recorder and then other instruments and get beyond horrific squawks to create sweet melodies.

What made her think she could make a difference by working at the elementary level where kids didn't have the option of taking her class or not? At least in the high school, music was an elective and only kids with at least a modicum of talent entered the band room.

It was her job to fan the embers of that tiny bit of interest and get kids excited about expressing themselves in music and dance.

At least she had a job. Server Boy was looking for something. Man, some days he could have hers, that was for sure. He'd be a hit with all the preteen girls in dance class.

~ ᶜ ᶜ

HIS DAD'S house was clean and ready for its new owners. Peyton had tried to help at first, but it seemed the emotion of leaving the only home she'd ever known overcame her, and she'd retreated to the backyard to have a good cry.

And then there was Beatrice, who'd refused to pick up a cleaning rag at all.

Seth hadn't had time to deal with Peyton's trauma or Beatrice's drama. Not when he'd needed to be ready to hand the keys over to the real estate agent by five o'clock.

The doorbell rang, and Garry Bertoli stuck his head around the door. "Ah, good. Looks all ready to go."

"Yes, sir." Seth pointed to the keys and final signed paperwork on the fireplace mantel. "I'll just go find the girls and be out of your hair. I hope the new owners will be very happy here."

He had mixed feelings himself. Yeah, there'd been good memories, but plenty of ugly ones had been sandwiched in the middle. At least he'd had the chance to make things right with his dad and ask forgiveness for his years of estrangement and rebellion.

"I'm sure they will be." Garry gave Seth's hand a firm shake. "Here's wishing you all the best in the future, and I hope you'll look me up when you're ready to buy."

What, in ten or twenty years? This man would probably have retired by then. "Thanks. I'll keep that in mind." Seth turned to the French doors that opened to the patio and fenced backyard. "Beatrice! Peyton! Time to go."

"I don't want to." Beatrice looked down from the big oak tree. "That stupid apartment doesn't even have a yard. Certainly not a climbing tree."

"The playground is half a block away, remember? And there are climbing trees by the river."

"Seth, do we have to?" Peyton's voice trembled.

His heart broke all over again for the two little girls. "I'm sorry. Truly. But our parents didn't leave enough money for us to keep this house."

"How come you don't have a job?" Beatrice hadn't moved from the limb above his head.

"Long story." With details no ten-year-old should attempt to process. "But I'm three-quarters through college, so things will look better after that."

"You're twenty-eight. College kids are like twenty."

"True enough. But I was a dropout when I was twenty." And again when he was twenty-eight, thanks to the sudden responsibility dumping on his shoulders a few weeks ago. He was going to do everything he could to finish off that degree in engineering, but it wasn't going to be easy. And, barring a major miracle, it wouldn't be this year.

His first assignment was keeping a roof over their heads and food on the table. Clothes for growing kids.

How this would have played out if he were still working at the bar just enough to keep him in party mode while he couch-surfed? Would he have accepted the responsibility of his sisters and straightened his life around?

No way to know. But he was thankful God had grabbed him eighteen months back and the transformation had already begun. It still seemed too little, too late. If the accident had happened a year later, Seth would have been set with that degree in hand and ready for a great job in an office building downtown.

Not that he loved canned air and no view, but whatever. The point was, he'd have had it made.

Beatrice swung over the limb and dropped to the ground then crossed her arms as she looked around the yard. "I guess we can go." Her lip trembled.

I feel you, kid. Seth nodded and reached for Peyton's hand. "How about we go past the drive-through and eat at the park by the river?" And man, did he need to hit the grocery store, which meant digging into his dwindling resources. Once the house funds hit his bank account, he could breathe again, but he wanted to save as much of that for the girls' education as he could.

He ushered the girls around the house and into his aging

car. A glance in the rearview mirror as he pulled away showed both girls staring back at the house with silent tears.

Seth cleared his throat, suspiciously scratchy itself. "Burgers or Chinese?" Chinese cost more, but this was a special occasion, right? The end of an era, and the beginning of a new one.

"Can I get a fortune cookie?" Peyton's voice brightened.

He managed to keep his fist pump contained. "Sure can, Pey. But what else? Ginger beef? Sweet-and-sour pork? Fried rice?"

The girls discussed what they liked and did not like all the way to the restaurant. Seth parked outside, ordered by phone, and waited until it was ready. Then he drove across the bridge and down to the riverside park.

Peyton lugged one of the paper bags over to a picnic table.

"What's that?" Beatrice asked, pointing out the lot next door that seemed loaded with trees, shrubs, and bushes.

Wait. That must be the food forest Wade had talked about. There wasn't anything else remotely resembling the description anywhere near the river. Seth looked down the street. Yes, there was Dixie and Dan's rental. This had to be the place. "I think it's a public garden of sorts."

Beatrice rolled her eyes. "Gardens have vegetables, not trees."

"Manito Park has flower gardens." Peyton peered into one of the paper containers. "Mmm, this smells yummy."

"You think we should learn to cook Chinese food at home?" Seth tore his attention from the rising hope in his chest at the glimpse of the food forest. They'd land on their feet. God would see to it. "We could have it more often if we made it ourselves."

Peyton gave a firm nod. "Count me in."

"How about you, Beatrice?"

"I guess." She opened another container and inhaled deeply. "Yeah, good idea."

This time Seth didn't hold the fist pump back. He and his sisters were going to be just fine.

5

*A*va leaned over the row of rhubarb plants in the food forest. Songbirds trilled in the morning sunshine, a few lazy honeybees landed on apple blossoms nearby, and the sun peeked into the valley.

It was easy to forget the stress of striving for another elementary school or two she could teach in for the next school year. Easy to forget the stress of working for Hailey North at the bistro. Thankfully, Ava mostly worked in the public side, not the kitchen, because Hailey had been grumpier than usual since Alex and Marley's wedding a couple of weeks ago.

Or maybe it was just Ava. She was grumpy, too, and Brittany's deepening relationship with Duncan didn't help at all. Nor did the wedding of Brittany's brother in a couple of days.

No. Ava was going to enjoy the sunshine today. Hailey had agreed to pay her for picking the rhubarb Bridgeview Bakery and Bistro would feature as long as supplies lasted.

Ava heard the voices before she saw them. Two girls

bickering. Great. Reminded her of the things she liked least about teaching. Preteen girls could be so petty. Could hurt each other so deeply over their power plays over — well, nothing, really.

The end of the school year was only a week away, and it couldn't come soon enough. When that arrived, Dominic and Katri's wedding would be over, as well, and only one more Santoro wedding — Tony and Kenna's — lingered on the horizon for Ava to attend with a smile.

"Don't be mean," one of the girls said in a teary voice.

"Don't be stupid," the other one shot back.

Why weren't rhubarb clumps tall enough to hide behind? But they weren't, and the raspberry brambles were too far away. Ava straightened, pasted on a smile, and turned toward the street. "Good morning, girls."

They looked about eight and ten or so. Not kids from the neighborhood or from one of Ava's schools. Who were they, then, wandering around Bridgeview unaccompanied if they didn't live here?

"Hi!" The younger one twirled in place then caught the eye of her sister and stopped, deflated.

"Nice dance move. I'm Ava. What's your name?" Seemed strange to give her first name instead of Ms. Santoro like the school kids knew her.

"Peyton D—"

"She's a stranger. We don't give our names to people we don't know." The older one crossed her arms and widened her stance as she stared, all but daring Ava to start something.

Ava couldn't help smiling at the challenge. "Wise words. Do you have a grownup with you?" They looked marginally old enough to roam unattended, but where had they come from?"

"Our brother is talking to Mr. Wade." Peyton pointed through the food forest toward the Ropers' house.

"He can see us from where he is," added the older girl.

"Great. Mr. Wade is a friend of mine." Was the girls' brother the guy Wade had been praying for? Cool of God to answer so quickly.

Ava bent over the bush again, tugging out another stalk of rhubarb. She deftly lopped off the giant leaf and used her knife to pull some of the fibrous strands to the other end of the stalk. Then she cut off the root ends and peeled off additional strands before putting the stalk in one pile and the trimmings on the other.

The younger girl stepped closer. "What is that?"

"Peyton..." warned the other.

"Rhubarb. I'd offer you a taste, but it's super tart when it's raw like this. Ms. Hailey at the bakery will add lots of sugar when she bakes muffins and desserts with it." Or monk fruit sweetener for some of the recipes, since they did a fairly brisk business in sugar-free and gluten-free desserts, thanks to one of the workers there. Ava's own sister-in-law, Sadie, had been the catalyst who encouraged Hailey and Kass to get on board with Astrid's zealous ideas. Sadie had lost over one hundred pounds in the year before her wedding to Peter by following the sugar-free Trim Healthy Mama way of eating. A gal would sure never guess to look at her now.

"We don't take food from strangers, either."

Touché.

The two girls stood a few feet away watching Ava work. She pulled several stalks from each plant. Good thing

Wade'd had the foresight to plant over a dozen of them. She knew better than to strip any clump down too far since that could kill it. She'd just gathered the leaves and trimmings into a pile to haul over to the compost bins when she heard Wade's voice.

"I see the girls have already found the place! Good morning, Ava. Thanks for taking care of the rhubarb."

"Hi, Wade." She looked up to give him a little wave, but froze. The guy standing next to Wade Roper was none other than Server Boy. Ah... make that Seth Donahue.

He'd been amazingly hot in black slacks and a white button-down the night of Alex and Marley's wedding, but so much more approachable — so much more real — in khaki shorts and a dark-gray T-shirt with an emblem on it she couldn't quite make out.

Wade's mouth moved, and Ava realized he was still talking. "— like you to meet Ava Santoro, who's volunteering in the project this summer. Ava, this is Seth Donahue. I've hired him to implement the requirements of the grant."

"Hi." She hated that her voice sounded all breathy.

Seth looked nearly as stunned but glanced toward the girls before looking back at her. "Pleased to meet you."

Oh. That's how he was going to play it? Like this was their first encounter? Well, didn't that mean she was as boring and forgettable as she'd dreaded?

He gestured toward the girls. "My sisters, Beatrice and Peyton."

"We've met." Sort of.

"Is she a stranger, Seth?"

Seth glanced at her then away before she could latch onto the contact. "Not if Mr. Wade vouches for her."

Wade laughed. "I definitely do. Ava is a well-respected

member of the community, and I've known her since she was a teenager. Now she's a teacher. You girls are going to be attending Bridgeview Elementary this fall, and Ava — I mean, Ms. Santoro — will be your music and dance teacher. Not only that, but she teaches some private dance classes all year round, and then, in her spare time, she works over at Bridgeview Bakery and Bistro." He pointed down the street.

Peyton clasped her hands in front of her. "Dance class? Oh, please, Seth. May I?"

"Sorry, pumpkin. It won't be possible." Seth sent an awkward smile in Ava's direction without looking in her eyes.

Great. Cutest guy she'd met in a while, best dance partner since she couldn't remember when, and he wasn't throwing off a single *interested* vibe.

HE'D HURT HER. He could see it on her face, not that he was looking. At least, he was trying not to. But how could a guy like him even dream of starting something with a woman like her? Look at the credentials Wade had rolled out on her behalf. A functioning and honored member of this community they'd just moved into. Someone who'd be teaching his sisters.

A gorgeous woman who looked glamorous even in jean shorts and a lacy pink tank top. Her hair was looped up in a more casual bun than she'd worn at the wedding, and her skin already looked a little tanned in late May. She was so far beyond anyone he could realistically date that the tightening in his gut was entirely ludicrous.

Not that dating anyone at all was in his future, at least not before he had finished college, found a decent job, and settled into this new life with Beatrice and Peyton.

"We'll leave you to it, Ava." Wade grinned at her as he turned back to Seth. "Let me show you where the project will go."

Seth fell into step beside him. "Are you sure it's okay if the girls come with me? I might be distracted, especially with the river so close. It's moving along pretty quickly past here."

"It's got a powerful current in the early part of the year, for sure. If you think they're responsible enough to stay away from it, I'm okay with you having them around. I know you can't afford childcare." Wade's face brightened. "Rebekah would probably love to have them around one day of the week. School's out next week. She's a counselor over at the elementary school — did I already tell you that? — and she'll be home with our munchkins for the summer. They're younger than your sisters. Olivia's not quite four, and Theodore is twenty-two months, but they love being outside, too."

"I couldn't impose."

"Don't worry about that. I'm sure Olivia and Theodore will love having other kids around. They're used to that with daycare."

"We'll see." Seth would have to drive the girls to and from school across the river for the next week, but that couldn't be helped. Not with the house closing so quickly and the apartment at Bridgeview Manor sitting vacant as though waiting for him like an answer to prayer.

He still wasn't used to that sort of thing. Not after the way he'd treated God for so many years. God ought to hold a grudge for a while at the very least. But Dixie, of all people, had reminded him of the story of the prodigal son and the party the father had thrown for him on his return. No grudges. Just a celebration.

Dixie hadn't known better before she found Jesus. Her life had been a total wreck from her childhood on.

Seth had been raised in Sunday school and church. His parents might not have been the most devoted believers — he could see that, looking back — but he'd learned the basics in his childhood. It wasn't God's fault Seth had shoved it all aside, though he'd blamed Him for his mother's death then Dad's quick marriage to a much younger woman. Lori's immediate pregnancy with Beatrice had disgusted Seth and sent him off the deep end.

Looking back, he'd been searching for an excuse. None of it was really Dad's fault. Yeah, God could have changed the course of history, so that was what Seth latched onto. Obviously, God didn't care, so bitterness set in.

It was hard getting past that, honestly.

Seth followed Wade past a row of juniper shrubbery and managed not to laugh. Great. What good were they in a food forest other than a conduit of bitterness? Oh, right. The berries could also be used to numb pain, another quality useful in gin production. Exactly what a good church guy like Wade was likely to promote. Seth choked back a snort.

He glanced over his shoulder. Peyton chattered away as she skipped along, carrying some leaves beside Ava, who had her own arms full. Beatrice wasn't visible, but Seth wasn't going to worry about that one. She was wary enough to take care of herself.

Wade explained the layout to Seth, who nodded along.

It wasn't a hard project, not for a guy used to working with his hands. It was just going to take some time and actual sweat. Outside. Could be a whole lot worse. And, while the pay wasn't excessive, it should be enough to keep Seth from dipping into reserves if he were careful.

No more Chinese takeouts or any other sort. So, yes, he'd be cooking at the end of a long day outdoors.

"By the way, Dan meant it when he offered Dixie for some childcare, too. She's got a big heart."

Yeah, she did. Seth could almost resent Dan at times. Seth had never stood a chance with Dixie, not when Dan stood patiently and prayerfully in the wings, waiting for Dixie to come to her senses and return to him and the kids.

"Oh, and I'll talk to Adriana Sheridan. Her daughter, Violet, is about the same age as Beatrice, and Adriana might be willing to have the girls over sometimes." Wade pointed to where the street curved away from the riverfront. "They live just over there, so it's close by, too."

Seth shook his head. "You don't have to do all this, you know. You hardly know me."

Wade clapped his hand on Seth's shoulder. "I'm a man who tries to listen to God's voice. You're a believer, right?"

A verbal reply was out of the question with the knots in Seth's throat, so he nodded.

"Then you know how it works. Sometimes God just lays something hard on a man's heart, and you know you have to do whatever it takes to move His plan along. God's got His hand on you, Seth Donahue, and I'm thrilled I get to be a part of it."

"Where do you get that kind of faith?"

Wade chuckled. "More than one or two hard knocks plus years of schooling by the good Lord."

"Well, thank you. I don't know what else to say."

"That's enough. Someday you'll be in a position to pay it forward, and that will be thanks enough for me."

An opportunity like that seemed impossibly far in the future. Seth looked over to the rhubarb row where Ava gathered ruby-red stalks into two large baskets. By the time he was solidly on his feet, Ava would be married and middle-aged with half a dozen kids.

And she'd still be gorgeous.

$\mathcal{T}$hat was a sweet wedding," Dafne said with a
wistful sigh.

"Yeah." Ava felt the same as they kicked off their heels
in the apartment she shared with Britt before Dominic and
Katri's reception.

"Katri's so pretty. So bubbly and fun."

"And her dress was to die for."

"Adriana sewed it, right? Maybe she can sew yours
someday."

"Or yours."

Dafne laughed. "Not as likely as you."

"Well, I'm sure all that lace and beading cost a pretty
penny. Not that Charlie would care or even notice. He
seems to enjoy spending money on everyone he loves."

"I'm happy Aunt Winnie snagged him." Dafne surged to
her feet and paced over to the window. "It seems strange to
have Gavin with a sitter all day today."

Ava watched her younger sister. "You leave at
daycare every day when you go to college or work."

"I know, but then I don't really have free time to miss him." Dafne twisted her hands as she turned to face Ava. "Do you think he'll be okay, growing up without a father?"

Hadn't they had this conversation before? Like, twenty times? "Yes, because you're amazing. And Dad and Peter are helping out to give him some male bonding. He'll be fine." Ava hesitated. "And one of these days you'll meet a nice guy, and then Gavin will get a dad."

"Right. Because decent men fall all over themselves to take on a girl with a kid."

"The right one will."

Dafne rolled her eyes. "Thanks for the nudge to become a teacher, though. When I'm through college and Gavin's in school, our schedules should mesh nicely, plus I should be able to afford to move out of Mom and Dad's basement."

"You know they don't mind having you there."

"I know. It just feels like everyone around me has had to give up so much because of my mistakes."

"Daf?"

"What?"

"You're good. You made one crappy choice—"

"At least two or three of them."

Ava laughed. "Okay, I'll grant that. But I've made stupid decisions, too, just not the same ones. Like going into teaching music and dance. How did I think that would create a steady job with reliable income? To say nothing of how most of the other elementary teachers are middle-aged women. The few male teachers I work with are married, like Myles."

"Teaching high school English should make me more secure once I find a job. Two more years, though."

"Yeah, we should have become nurses like Katri. Lots of

hot guys in a hospital. Doctors. Nurses. Lab techs. Way more options."

"You're calling our cousin hot?" Dafne bobbed her eyelashes.

"Katri seems to think so. I can't believe Dominic is a year younger than I am, and he's already a fully qualified medical doctor. Makes me feel like such a slacker."

"Oh, stop it. You chose a different path, that's all. You were plenty smart enough to become a doctor if you wanted."

"But... blood." Ava shuddered.

"Exactly. And super nasty hours."

"Right." She eyed her younger sister. "I hate weddings, you know that? I'm so tired of all the hoopla and everyone going around with blissfully happy smiles. There's still Tony and Kenna's wedding to survive then nobody else for a while, right?"

"Not that I know of." Dafne settled into a deep chair and checked her watch. "Almost time for the reception. Keep your chin up a little longer."

"I tried to talk Hailey into letting me serve at the reception."

"You didn't."

"I did. But she said she had plenty of staff to cover it."

"Is that hot guy you danced with working it, you think?"

Ava hadn't told her sister she'd run into Seth again, that he was working for Wade and had two little sisters he seemed to be caring for. She shrugged. "I don't know." She'd practically bit her tongue off to keep from asking, though.

"Do you think there's anything between Hailey and Basil?" Dafne asked.

"I wondered the same thing at Alex's wedding. They

seemed to be pretty intense. But that's crazy, isn't it? They're both, like, over thirty. Why wouldn't they just go out with each other if they had feelings?"

"No idea. The whole thing seems a little bizarre if you ask me. I wouldn't date Basil if he were the last guy on earth. And, you know, not my cousin."

"I hear you, girl. I was surprised to see him at the church this afternoon after how snide he was about weddings when we were paired together at Alex and Marley's."

"He and Dominic spent some time together in Seattle the past couple of years, I guess."

"That must be it." Ava pursed her lips. "Unless he's here to see Hailey."

Dafne laughed. "Yeah, right. Anyway, we should head over to the community center. It's nearly time."

It was only a couple of blocks away, so they walked over. There were plenty of vehicles parked along the street as it was. The nearer they got, the faster Ava walked.

"Girl, slow down. My feet are killing me."

"Sorry."

Dafne eyed her. "You may not know he's serving, but you're hoping."

"Nah." Yes. Totally.

"I don't believe you. Why not ask him out if he's here?"

"He won't be here." Pretty sure not, anyway. "And I was raised better than that. As were you."

"Whatever. It's the twenty-first century, and there's nothing wrong with making your interest clear."

Ava also wasn't ready to tell her sister she knew where Seth could be found most weekdays. It had been all she could do to avoid the food forest during working hours this past week. Dafne had a point, though. Why not talk to him and see if it went anywhere?

Yeah, no. Not with two little girls listening in. And Seth didn't even have a job besides this temporary one. What kind of future would that be? Just because the guy was hot — and he definitely was — didn't mean she shouldn't hold out for a man equally hot but in a better situation in life. She should ask Dominic if he could introduce her to any young single doctors.

The community center doors were propped open to the late May sunshine as the sisters entered. Ava stepped to the side to allow her eyes a chance to adjust to the relative dimness.

Dafne's elbow caught her ribs. "He's here."

Ava peeked toward the food tables across the space just as Seth set down a large, heavy-looking platter. The white button-up strained slightly with his movement. His jaw tensed with focus. Every blond hair was in place.

Her breath caught. Eye candy. That's all he was. She didn't know enough about him to fall for him. Everything she did know screamed at her to stay away, but when Dafne hooked their arms together and dragged her between the long tables garnished with white tablecloths and grand flower-and-candle arrangements, she didn't resist.

"Oh, this food looks delish. Right, Ava?" Dafne dropped her arm and looked at her pointedly as they stopped in front of the luscious spread.

"Mmm, sure does." But Ava couldn't keep her gaze off Seth Donahue. His intense eyes stared right back at her, and for an instant, she was back at Alex's wedding, dancing in Server Boy's arms. "Hi, Seth." That hadn't come out firm at all. She cleared her throat.

He grinned for a second before he straightened his back. "Hi, Ava." Then he pivoted and headed back into the kitchen.

"He's totally into you," Dafne whispered.

Looked more like polite rejection from Ava's point of view.

SETH FOCUSED on his work for the next couple of hours. He set out plates, refilled the punchbowl and platters, removed plates, and ran the dishwasher, all without being alone with Hailey and without meeting Ava Santoro's eyes. He felt as though Ava's gaze followed him, but he didn't dare check.

She was way too good for him. He knew it, even if she didn't... yet. As for Hailey, he wasn't going to be used to make another man jealous. Not blatantly like she seemed to be into.

When the tables had been folded and stored and the string quartet ramped up for the dance, Seth slipped out the backdoor into the twilight. He leaned against the side of the brick building for a minute and massaged his temples. The things he did for money, but this was better than some of the jobs he'd had before.

Lord, You've set me on a difficult path. I realize it's not the hardest one known to mankind, but it's tough, just the same.

He walked away, and the music faded. He took the steps down to the street below and headed toward Dan and Dixie's house. Dixie served at Antonio's three nights a week, but Dan had offered to keep the girls so Seth could work the reception.

How did he deserve friends like these? Especially Dan,

whom Seth only knew through hitting on Dixie in his darkest days. But Dan had welcomed him with open arms when he'd asked forgiveness and seemed determined to be a true friend.

Dan reminded Seth of Jesus. His big heart, his ability to forgive, his staunch willingness to do what he could for those who needed help. Those like Seth.

Seth knew better than to ring the doorbell when it was past little Henry's bedtime. He let himself into the house and looked through to the dining room table where the three girls sat coloring printouts of unicorns with gel pens. Even Beatrice looked to be having a good time. Well, at least she wasn't scowling. That was a start.

"Hey, reception over already?" Dan glanced at the clock.

"The dance is on, and Hailey's core group will do the midnight lunch."

"Fair enough. The boys are in bed. Want to grab a pop and sit out on the back deck a bit? The girls aren't done coloring their pictures yet." Dan smoothed Mandy's messy curls, and his stepdaughter grinned up at him.

Guy talk? Absolutely. "You girls okay with that?"

Peyton nodded and Beatrice ignored him. He'd take that as affirmative.

Dan grabbed two cans of pop from the fridge and led the way out to the patio. "This is the best thing about this house." He settled into a deep Adirondack chair. "Love this big covered area and the fenced-in yard. We're saving to buy a place, though."

"Yeah, this is a nice spot. Beats the apartment all to bits."

Dan chuckled. "I bet. Well, come down anytime you like. Seriously."

"Thanks." Seth took a gulp of his cola. "Got a question for you."

"Hmm?"

"I don't know if I'm doing the right thing by Beatrice and Peyton. Would they be better off in foster care than with a broke, single guy like me?"

"I doubt it."

"And then there's their aunt. She told me at the funeral she wants custody, but then I haven't heard anything more."

Dan leaned forward, elbows on his knees. "Oh? Does she know them well? What's her situation?"

"You think I should give them up to her."

"I didn't say that. But maybe? If she'd be a good fit. It would sure make your life easier. The girls, too?"

"I don't know." Seth started to run his hand through his hair and stabbed himself with stiff gel. Was he clinging to them for the right reasons? Could he atone for anything in his life by caring for his sisters? "There's something about Lori's sister and brother-in-law I don't trust, but the girls do need a mom. A woman."

"You could get married."

"Oh, yeah. Just snap my fingers and find the right girl? No one would want me, especially now." Not a good woman, anyway. Not someone like Ava.

"You know I'm not Mandy's or Buddy's dad, right?"

Seth nodded. He'd heard the story.

"I fought hard to keep those kids when Dixie left me."

"To hear her tell the story, you kicked her out."

Dan was quiet so long Seth wondered if he'd crossed a line. "It was a really rough time. Not gonna lie. She was way off the deep end."

Seth remembered. He'd met Dixie at a drinking party at

Billie and Jared's right around then. When he and Diana had been on the outs. "Why did you fight for her kids?"

"Well, I didn't want them to be separated. Henry's mine, but Mandy and Buddy are his half-siblings. They belong together, you know? And I love them. But I wasn't sure I was doing the right thing, either."

"Oh?"

Dan eyed him. "If you're seriously wondering — if you have questions about custody and stuff — you should see an attorney. Sadie Santoro is a good one. Family law is her specialty."

"Man, I can't afford a lawyer." And did he want a Santoro attorney? Probably not.

"I couldn't, either. Sadie took me on pro bono. Want me to talk to her and see if she'll do the same for you? A consult or two?"

Seth wasn't likely to get a better offer. "Yeah, maybe. It's not that I don't want them. It's just... I'm terrified it's the wrong choice, and I'll wreck their lives. What do I know about preteens — girls, especially?"

"I felt the same about Mandy, and she was only five. You've got one nearly ready to bloom."

A jolt of panic rammed through Seth. "I can't do this. I really can't."

"Let me talk to Sadie. I think... honestly, Seth? If you open the door to their aunt, and it doesn't work out, that might get Child Protective Services involved, and they might wind up in foster care anyway. It might put them on someone's radar. Then you'd have no control over their placement. There are a lot of good foster homes, but not all of them. And they might be split up, too. That was a big fear of mine with Mandy and Buddy."

Seth drove his hands through his hair, dislodging the gel he'd carefully applied a few hours back. "I know. I know. I just wish my dad and Lori hadn't been on that flight. The girls need their parents, not me."

"But you're what they've got." Dan bumped his shoulder gently. "You know what else? You've got Jesus on your side. That will make all the difference."

7

The rhubarb wasn't coming in as quickly as it had a week or two ago. Ava looked at the meager pile she'd picked then looked around the food forest. The strawberries were looking good, but not quite ready yet. She adjusted the netting over their beds as two of the chickens scrounged for bugs nearby.

This would be her last early morning here, now that the rhubarb was over. She should ask Wade what else she could do. Or she could admit she was here to see Seth... except not, or she'd come a little later. What kind of game was going on in her head?

"Morning, Ava."

She jumped. Whirled. "Seth. Good morning. You're early."

"I thought I'd get started before the day gets too warm. I've got a lot of digging to do."

"No little sidekicks?"

He shook his head. "Not today. They're over at the Sheridans'."

"Oh, I guess Beatrice and Violet are close to the same age." And Adriana certainly had a big enough heart to help out with someone else's kids.

"Beatrice is a year younger, but yeah. Pretty close." Seth's hands flexed at his side. "I should get going."

"What exactly is your assignment?" His words had probably been a hint that Ava should say goodbye and leave him to it. But school was out now for the summer, and she had some free time this morning. She'd take the rhubarb to the bistro when she worked the noon rush.

"Wade got a permit to pump water from the river. Most of what's in here doesn't need more water than falls from the sky, but he wanted to add a boggy area and some in-ground water lines just in case."

"And a pond and stream, right? I think I heard something about this project."

He nodded. Looked away.

That meant she could stare for a minute. Those blond strands looked a little damp and tousled compared to his gelled Server Boy look. He wore long jeans and shoes, probably a good idea for digging. His gray T-shirt clung to his chest... Ava's perusal stalled on his forearm. A tattoo? She couldn't edge close enough to see it clearly without being totally obvious.

A tattoo, though. Her perfect guy wouldn't have one of those. He'd be so clean-cut and spiritual he'd practically squeak.

Something stabbed her conscience. Did that mean there was no room in her life for someone who was redeemed later than infancy? For someone who'd wandered at all? Maybe it did. Was that so wrong? Maybe she was being rather judgy. But was she just trying to make exceptions because she reacted so strongly to Seth? Emotions. Such complicated things.

That forearm moved, shifting across Seth's chest.

Her gaze jolted to meet his, and he offered a sardonic grin. "Never seen ink before?"

"I, uh, yes, of course, I have." *Jump in, Ava.* "I just couldn't figure out what yours is from this angle. At first I thought it was a treble clef, but I can see now it isn't."

"You're right. It's actually a Celtic symbol."

The guy was full of surprises. She raised her eyebrows. "Of what?"

"Joy. Embracing life." An expression crossed his face and slipped away before she could analyze it.

"That seems... odd."

"Why?" He crossed his arms, cutting off her full view. "Seem a little girly to you?"

Ava's face flushed, giving away her reaction in a heartbeat.

"I lived for myself for too many years." His voice was emotionless. "I have a few tattoos with less stellar meanings. My thoughts and actions embraced darkness rather than light. I got this ink partly to cover up a small marking I didn't want to display anymore, but mostly to remind myself that I've made a choice for Jesus. I choose to embrace life. I choose to find joy."

And here she'd been judging him. "That's actually really cool." For the first time, the thought of getting a tattoo herself dashed through her mind without being shot full of holes. Still, no.

"You think?"

Hadn't she said so? Ava nodded.

"It's hard to reprogram my brain." He plucked a green

berry from a nearby juniper shrub and held it up. "It tends to bitterness, like juniper. Choosing joy — embracing life — is a constant decision."

"I... I don't know what to say." Was he talking about depression? Ava's life had been pretty even-keeled. Yeah, she'd rocked a bit here and there, but she'd been raised by loving parents in the church and had absorbed their teaching since she was a child. Life was good, most of the time. A disappointment here and there, sure, but nothing deep and lasting like depression. From what she'd heard, there was little choice involved in it.

He chuckled. "That's a start."

"What do you mean?"

"So many people assume a little willpower and a little prayer is all that's needed to forever vanquish the darkness. They're happy to spout that unhelpful viewpoint to anyone who suffers."

Ava winced. Just because she hadn't said it out loud didn't mean she hadn't thought it. "It's not something I know much about—"

"Thank God for that. I mean those words sincerely, not sarcastically. It's not a fun road." Seth looked away. "I really should get started here today."

"Do you need a hand?" Ava resisted the impulse to slap her palm over her mouth. The words were already out.

He glanced over her. "You're not dressed for dirt."

"I could be in ten minutes." She pointed up the metal stairs beneath the overhead bridge. "I only live a couple of blocks away."

"I know."

Ava had bent to pick up the rhubarb but now she

straightened and pinned Seth with a narrowed look. "You know where I live?"

He nodded, and his chest filled with a deep breath. "I overheard you in the stairwell one day talking to someone."

She crossed her arms. "You live in Bridgeview Manor?"

Seth rubbed his temple. "Just moved in a couple of weeks ago."

Wait. What? He'd lived there for two weeks and she hadn't even noticed? There were twelve apartments, four on each floor, so she didn't know everyone well, but to think he'd been so near and she'd never guessed! So much for her plan to take cookies to the new neighbors.

"My cousin and I live in 302. And you?"

He had the grace to look abashed. "202."

"You're right beneath us."

"Yeah."

"And you knew." Ava wasn't sure if she should be ticked off or honored that he cared enough to remember. It wasn't like he owed her anything.

"Look, you said it best a minute ago. I'm beneath you." Seth held up a hand. "I know you meant apartments, but it's still true. I'm just a college dropout who's made a mess of his life and suddenly finds himself responsible for two kids. I... I like you, Ava Santoro, but I have nothing but friendship to offer."

That was a boatload of brutal honesty. She studied him until he looked at her again. Then she stuck out her hand. "I always need more friends."

He shook it firmly then stepped away, his gaze still locked on hers. "Thanks. Me, too."

Had he not even felt the warm jolt when their hands clasped? Had he not even noticed the thrill when they danced together a few weeks ago? But maybe he was right. Maybe friendship was the best idea.

After all, she was looking for Mr. Perfectly Right, and Seth wasn't him.

TRUE TO HER WORD, Ava returned shortly, hair braided back, dressed in jeans and work boots along with a no-nonsense black tank top. She tugged on a pair of leather work gloves. "I've only got until ten-fifteen. Then I need to shower and be at the bistro by eleven. I've got a shift over lunch."

Brisk. Ready to work. That made it easier, since Seth had spent the intervening time terrified she'd come back and equally terrified she wouldn't. "Okay, that's three hours. Can you help me lay out the line down to the river? I wish Wade had thought of this before planting all those trees because it would have been far easier to dig a trench with a Bobcat than by hand."

"But then you wouldn't have a job."

"There's that." He chuckled.

"If you need a Bobcat, though, I know someone who's got one."

"So do I. Dan Ranta. He's got a landscaping service."

"Right. That's who I was thinking of." Ava grabbed the measuring tape he held out. "Want me to stay right here while you head to where you want it to come out?"

"Sure." He tucked several stakes under his arm and backed away with the rolling end. "How do you know Dan?"

"Well, first, in Bridgeview, everyone knows everyone.

Unless someone sneaks into their apartment building and doesn't let others know they live there."

He grinned as he dropped a stake where he needed to angle the line. "Yeah, I can see how that would mess with your pretty little head." Drat, he was going to stop flirting with her. He was. Unless Dan was right about other things, like getting married.

"Also, Dan's sister is a good friend of my cousin Jasmine — never mind. Just go with everyone knows everyone, and you'll get the picture."

"Must make it hard to be a rebel." Seth eyed the next section. Still not a straight run to the river when he needed to dodge tree roots.

"I wouldn't know. I've never tried it."

Of course, she hadn't. Just as he suspected.

"On the other hand, my cousin Basil managed," she went on. "He hid a drinking problem for years before he got careless and ran a police checkpoint with Dixie in the car—"

Seth glanced up just in time to see her slap a hand over her mouth.

"And, well, Dixie's come to the Lord since then, but Basil is still a free spirit. He paid his fine, did his jail time, and relinquished his driver's license for two years. But I'm not sure he learned anything."

Basil. Wasn't that the guy Ava had been with when he'd first seen her? The one Hailey North had been pretending not to ogle. "Didn't he move away, though? If I'm thinking of the right guy."

"Seattle." Ava sighed. "That likely tells you how hard it is to be a rebel and live in Bridgeview, especially if you're a

Santoro. Our nonna sees everything and knows everything and has an opinion about everything."

"Nonna... is that your grandmother?" Seth tapped in another stake. "I don't remember mine."

"Oh, that's too bad. I mean, I'm not super close to her, not like some of my cousins. To me she just seems like she's in it for the meddling, but that's probably not fair. I know she prays for each of us every day."

"And Basil twice on Sunday?"

Ava giggled.

Seth stilled and looked up at her. With every word out of her mouth, he fell for her just a little more. Why couldn't he get it through his thick skull that she was irrevocably out of bounds? She'd even said it herself in a roundabout way. She didn't have a rebellious bone in her body. Likely that grandmother of hers rightly knew Ava wasn't the grandkid she needed to worry about going all crazy and falling for a guy like Seth. A guy with a past.

He was just an interesting enigma to a girl like Ava. A teacher. A dancer. A beautiful, secure woman who didn't rock the boat — didn't need to, because she already had everything she wanted and needed.

Seth cleared his throat. "I'm going to start digging." He strode over to where he'd left the tools Wade had loaned him and picked up a shovel. He wedged the tip into the ground and jumped on the shoulders to ram it in as deeply as he could on the first try.

"Want me to spray the line with the flagging paint?"

"Sure. That would be a help." He'd have thought of it himself if her presence hadn't rattled him so much.

Ava leaned beside him, spray can in hand.

He inhaled her fragrance. Gardenias, like she'd worn to

the wedding. Then he stopped breathing for a few seconds so he wouldn't suck in paint fumes.

She worked her way toward the first stake, and he settled back on his heels to watch her. Bad idea, but if friendship was the only card he held, he could at least remember what she looked like.

At the first stake, she glanced back at him, and he looked away. She'd caught him again. But his resolve still held. She was too good for him. Way, way too good.

Dan's idea of a marriage of convenience to keep custody was totally unhelpful.

$a$driana Sheridan met him at the carport door when he'd finally put in his eight hours. "Hi, Seth. The girls are out back playing with the dog."

He raised an eyebrow. "You call that a dog? Looks more like a small pony."

"Duke?" Adriana laughed. "Good thing we have a large lot, right? He's part golden Lab, part Great Pyrenees, and part who-knows-what. We got him from the pound when Violet was a baby."

"He seems to be doing well for his age."

"He is. Want to come in for a glass of iced tea before taking the girls home?"

Seth looked down at his jeans and T-shirt. He'd dusted off as much as he could, but he was far from clean.

"Oh, don't worry about a little dirt. I've got three kids and a monster of a dog. Trust me, this house has seen dirt before." She turned into the house. "Sam, call Dad and let him know Mr. Seth is here."

"I don't want to be a bother," Seth hedged.

"Never a bother to get to know a new neighbor." She stepped back and held the door for him.

He'd be rude to protest further, even though all he really wanted was a shower and a sandwich. He followed his hostess into a spacious and beautiful house. The kitchen to his left revealed an expanse of granite countertops with a tray of cooling cookies. His stomach rumbled just a little, hopefully too quietly for her to hear. To the right, a long table with a floral arrangement in the center stretched toward French doors. A wooden highchair sat in the corner. The whole place looked elegant at the same time it looked lived in.

"Seth Donahue?" A man entered from the hallway. "I'm Myles Sheridan, Adriana's husband."

Seth clasped the man's hand. "Pleased to meet you. Your wife was kind enough to offer to watch my sisters..."

"Anything to help a neighbor." Myles pointed out the French doors. "The girls have been outside for hours. That's made Sam here very happy, since his sister would have been bugging him to climb trees with him if Beatrice and Peyton weren't present."

Sam looked to be about thirteen, a scraggly boy who made Seth think of Harry Potter with his dark hair and glasses. The boy held up a thick hardcover. "Almost done reading my book."

Adriana squeezed the boy to her side. "Does that mean a trip to the library tomorrow?"

He grinned. "Please?"

"I'll take you," Myles said. "I need to do a bit of research anyway."

"Why don't you guys go out on the back deck, and I'll bring out a tray?" suggested Adriana.

A tray sounded good, like maybe some of those cookies might be coming his direction. And this way, Seth could see the girls before he had to call them to leave their new friend's house.

"I'll help you, Mom." Sam laid his hardcover face down on the table and followed his mother into the kitchen.

That was the kind of kid Seth hoped to raise. Someone the polar opposite of Beatrice — polite and helpful without being coerced. Seth trailed Myles out onto a wide covered deck with an array of comfortable seating. The fully fenced backyard extended a long way down to where the river raged just beyond.

He heard Peyton's voice coming from a treehouse toward the other end of the property as he took a seat. "Nice place you have here. It's hard to believe we're in the middle of the city."

"It is very peaceful. I can't take any credit for it, though. Adriana and her first husband, Sam and Violet's father, bought it. Stephan died when the kids were quite young. I've only been in the picture for three years or so now."

Seth tried to hold back the whiplash as he turned to look at the other man. "But Sam calls you Dad."

Myles gave a lopsided grin. "I'm thankful for it every day, but it's his choice. Violet was a lot harder to win over."

The girl seemed more... volatile. Seth had only met Violet a couple of times briefly, but there wasn't enough to make him turn down Adriana's offer. He'd have to watch his sisters — Beatrice, especially — for a negative attitude after being around Violet. A *more* negative attitude than she already sported.

Sam came out the door hauling a toddler and plopped him in Myles's lap. "Jamie wants you, Dad."

Adriana was right behind her son with a tray containing a large pitcher of tea, several empty glasses, and an open container.

Whew, she wasn't going to be chintzy with those cookies.

Sam draped an arm over his mom's shoulders and stretched his other hand toward the tin. "How many may I have?"

She swatted his hand away. "None. You already snuck a stack onto a plate in the kitchen. Don't think I didn't see you."

Sam laughed. "Can't blame a guy for trying. Nice to meet you, Mr. Seth." And he turned back into the house.

They'd seemed like such a normal family, but only the toddler belonged to Myles? There must be a story there, maybe a lot of story, not that it was any of Seth's business.

Adriana poured a glass for her husband and then Seth before holding out the container toward them. Not only the oatmeal cookies he'd seen on the cooling rack, but brownies, too? He took one of each.

"My wife loves to cook and bake," Myles said with a chuckle as he handed an oatmeal cookie to the toddler snuggled against his chest. "Lucky me, but it keeps me working out."

"I bet." Seth took a bite of the brownie. "Wow, thanks, Adriana. This is really good."

"I'm glad you like it." She smiled and took her own seat. "The girls will be in Bridgeview Elementary this fall? You live in the catchment, right?"

He nodded. "Yes. I need to figure out how to transfer them in."

"I can help with that." Myles took a sip. "I teach second

grade there. Peyton's finished second, right? So, I won't teach either of your sisters."

Seth blinked. "You teach elementary?'

"Sure, why not? I've always loved kids." Myles gave a soft smile to his wife. "Never thought I'd have any of my own, so it seemed a natural choice for me."

"Cool." And why couldn't men teach preteens? Seth had never thought much about it, but all the teachers he remembered from his younger years were female. With so many kids raised in fatherless homes these days, a male teacher could make a big difference. Maybe that had been part of it for Myles and Adriana.

"Ava Santoro gave you a hand today at the project?" Myles asked.

Another case of whiplash. "Uh, yeah?" How did the man know? Not that the food forest was exactly hidden.

"I biked by this morning. She's a great addition to the team at Bridgeview Elementary. The kids are far better off getting their music class from her than from me, I can tell you that right now."

His wife chuckled. "Violet loves her, and that takes some doing. The dance classes Ava holds over at the church are popular with a lot of the neighborhood kids."

"At the... church?"

"Yes, there's a great space for it in the basement. Sam's thing is voice, and Ava's tutored him a lot in that, as well. She has a way of getting the best out of the kids, and they don't even notice how hard they're working."

"That's great." What else was he supposed to say? They couldn't possibly know Ava had caught his attention beyond working together today at the permaculture project. Were they matchmaking or just enthusing about the one person they knew he knew in the neighborhood?

"Seth?" Peyton stood in front of him, clasping her hands together and batting her eyelashes.

She wanted something. He wouldn't tell her she was so totally obvious he was already braced. She'd figure out soon enough that she was giving him fair warning. "Hey, pumpkin. How was your day?"

"Good." She glanced at Adriana. "Thanks, Mrs. Sheridan."

"You're welcome, sweetie. You and your sister can come over any time." Adriana nodded at Seth. "Really."

"Can we go to dance class? I mean, I'm not sure Beatrice wants to, but please, please, *please* can I? Violet says it's so fun."

"I—" He couldn't flat out say no in front of these neighbors, but there was no money in the budget for any extras like that. "We'll have to see. Maybe after school starts in the fall." If he could find a job.

Peyton quivered her lower lip at him pitifully.

Was that on purpose or was she simply overcome with emotion? Talk about a crash course in dealing with young girls.

"Oh, that's a great idea," put in Adriana. "Violet will go on Thursday afternoons now that school's out for the summer. They're preparing a routine for Labor Day weekend to introduce the new Sunday school year."

"I can't—"

"Will you be coming to Sunday school at Bridgeview Bible Church?"

"Uh…"

"You really should. Wade told us you're a believer, and

that's a great community church. Pastor Tomas is terrific, and I think you'll love it. They have Junior Church over the summer — Peyton's young enough to go — and then Sunday school for all ages starts after Labor Day."

Seth felt like a tsunami was threatening to wash him away, but he needed to hold his ground before he agreed to something just to stop the flood. "I'll keep it in mind."

Myles chuckled. "You've overwhelmed him, love."

"No, it's—"

"You have that deer-caught-in-the-headlights look, Seth. Adriana's not that different from Violet. Sure she knows what everyone else wants."

Adriana made a face at her husband before turning to Seth. "Sorry."

"It's fine. I know getting the girls back into church is important. It is for me, too. Everything has just been so paralyzing the past few weeks I've backburnered that one."

Jamie slid off Myles's lap and toddled over to Peyton, grabbing at her leg.

"Aw, he's so cute. I always wanted a little brother."

This time Peyton's teary eyes didn't look fake, but it wasn't a desire Seth could fulfil, thank the Lord. Their dad and Lori had decided two was enough. Probably Dad had begun to realize what age he'd be when these two were teens. He'd had no way of knowing he'd pass away before that became an issue.

Seth reached for Peyton, and she leaned against his shoulder.

"You can come play with Jamie any time you want." Adriana looked between them. "Anytime that's okay with your brother."

He smoothed Peyton's messy hair and mouthed *thank*

you to Adriana over the girl's head.

"Pey-*ton*!" yelled Beatrice from the treehouse.

"Can I go play some more? Violet's tree fort is really cool. There's no boys allowed."

Seth bet Sam was just as glad that was true. "Fifteen minutes. Then please, both of you come right away when I call, okay?"

"Okay." She scampered off and clambered gracefully up the rope ladder. She'd blossom with dance classes.

Adriana removed the lid from a toy chest beside the railing and little Jamie all but dove in. Then she glanced back at her husband before refocusing on Seth. "We'd like to invite you for dinner Sunday after church." She held up a hand. "You don't have to visit ours or anywhere at all. It's just when the meal will be. But we often have a group of friends over on Sunday afternoons, and we'd like to help you get to know your neighbors. Please say you and the girls will come."

"Thank you." Seth squashed back the question of whether Ava was invited. Just friends, remember? That's all he had to offer.

Maybe he should look into how much her dance classes cost before he made a firm refusal. Maybe it wasn't too much if it made Peyton and Beatrice happy — not that anything really had that effect on Beatrice, but he could hope, right? And maybe it would be worth the expense to regularly see Ava in her natural element. He couldn't count on her coming by the project every day for all they'd worked well together.

Seth really should put Ava completely out of his mind, but if innocent daydreams were all he would ever had, was it so wrong to indulge?

9

I'm sorry. Brittany had other plans."

"Oh, too bad." Adriana shook her head with a smile. "Maybe another time. I didn't give her much notice."

Right. Which meant Ava was the pathetic one without a life. Still, an invitation to Myles and Adriana's for Sunday lunch was highly sought after. Adriana had once planned to turn dinners at her house into a business before she'd met Myles and become understandably sidetracked.

Adriana held the door wider. "Come on through. Nearly everyone is out on the back deck. Just follow the noise."

"Can I give you a hand?" The aromas from the magazine-worthy kitchen tantalized Ava.

"I don't..." Adriana studied her for a few seconds. "You know what? Sure. Sam has set up the self-serve area on the deck, and Myles is about to start grilling burgers. But I could use a hand wrapping the asparagus with bacon, if you're up for that? Then I'll finish the spring greens."

"I'd love to." Ava washed up at the kitchen's secondary sink and turned to the items laid out on the island for assembly. A few had been done. It looked pretty straightforward. "Who all is here today?"

"Rebekah and Wade. Dixie and Dan. Seth Donahue and his sisters. Myles mentioned you've met Seth?"

Ava's breath stuttered. "Um, yes. A couple of times." Hadn't Adriana and Myles been at Alex and Marley's wedding? Maybe Ava's dance with Seth hadn't caught every eye in Bridgeview after all.

"He knows the Rantas, and he's working for Wade. But I really wanted to give him a chance to get to know some of the teachers over at the school, like Myles and Rebekah and you."

So, it wasn't a matchmaking attempt. That should feel like more of a relief than it did. Like even the folks in the neighborhood thought Ava would be too hard to please... and hadn't noticed her infatuation with Seth Donahue.

"Did you hear that Lisa Brunner is retiring?"

"No! Really?" Mrs. Brunner taught fifth grade and was one of Ava's favorite teachers to work with. "I didn't think she was that old."

"Her husband was just offered an early retirement package. They bought a big RV and plan to travel full-time." Adriana gave Ava a significant look. "You should apply for her job."

"But... then I couldn't teach music." Tempting, though. It would give her a full-time position. Someone else could fight their way through finding five different schools to make being an elementary music teacher feasible.

"I know. I just wanted to be sure you knew it was a possibility. Randi Nordstrom would hire you in a heartbeat."

Ava wasn't quite that sure the Bridgeview Elementary

principal would take a chance on a newbie teacher. "I'll think about it."

Rebekah Roper appeared in the doorway. "Hey, ladies! What can I do to help? Wade and Dan have Theodore, Jamie, and Henry down by the sandbox."

"Hiya." Ava smiled a greeting to the elementary school counselor. That crew of little boys weren't far apart in age.

"Sure. Would you mind slicing the tomatoes and cheese for the burgers? Everything's set out across from Ava."

Ava shifted the bowl of asparagus closer. "I don't need all this space. I'm nearly done here."

Rebekah leaned closer. "Looks good." She glanced toward the French doors, which stood ajar on the far side of the dining room. "Question for you, Ava."

"Hmm?" She wrapped a strip of bacon around three skinny asparagus stalks.

"Your Thursday dance class. Is it full, or do you have room for two more?"

Ava thought fast. "I could add two more, but that would be the max. I'd originally hoped for sixteen kids so we could shift partners and groups during the performance. It's a little more complex with the fourteen I have now."

"Then if I paid for the Donahue girls—?"

"I'll pay for one," Adriana interrupted.

Ava looked between them. Wow, Seth and his sisters had already gained a staunch cheering squad. "I guess it depends on if Seth would accept the charity." The girls had seemed eager the other day — Peyton, at least — but he'd lacked enthusiasm.

"Do you think it would be better to announce it in front of everyone so he can't back out?" Adriana looked between them. "Or be a little more subtle?"

Rebekah laughed. "You wouldn't know subtle if it bit you in the backside."

"I could try." Adriana chuckled. "What do you think, Ava?"

"No clue. You're not dragging me into this."

"You might know him better than any of us." Rebekah tipped her head and studied Ava. "Don't think I haven't looked out the window and seen you working with him in the food forest."

"Oh?" Adriana's gaze sharpened.

Busted. "He needed a hand a few times is all. And look, I'm done wrapping these. Are they going out to the grill?" Because maybe she could escape.

"No, under the broiler in here. Why don't you go check with Myles? We'll need his five-minute warning for when to start."

"Sure." Ava turned to the hand sink, waiting for the two women to make further comments, but they were uncharacteristically silent. Towel in hand, she glanced back at them, only to see them looking at each other with raised eyebrows. If she didn't think they were talking about her, she'd laugh at their undeniable silent dialogue.

She made her escape to the back deck, though it wouldn't likely be much of a reprieve. Girlish voices came from the treehouse. As Rebekah had said, a few of the men lounged on the lawn with the toddlers nearby. Buddy Ranta and Olivia Roper yanked a toy truck back and forth until Dixie smoothly intervened.

Seth sat near Myles and Sam beside the grill. All three looked up as Ava stepped through the doors. Myles rose. "Is this my signal?"

Ava tore her gaze from Seth to Myles. "Adriana asked for a five-minute warning for the asparagus."

"And I'm still waiting for the directive to start grilling."

Sam bounded to his feet. "I'll go check with Mom."

Ava shifted to let the boy pass, which put her near Seth.

Myles smirked. "Are you still helping out at the food forest?" He toggled his grill brush between them.

"I... sometimes?" Ava glanced at Seth and found herself locked into his eyes, not for the first time. It was like he wore magnets for contact lenses.

"Great. Everyone needs a helping hand at times." But Myles's voice seemed to come from a distance.

⁓⁓⁓

Wow. As always when he was near Ava, Seth found himself tongue-tied and fuzzy-headed, like back when he'd been fourteen and had a crush on one of the cheerleaders. He hadn't even hit his growth spurt yet. No popular girl gave him a second look for another couple of years.

He bet Ava could have been on the cheer squad with her lithe form. Those klutzy moments the night they'd first met didn't seem to represent the real Ava. She was gorgeous and perfect in every way.

And he was staring.

Seth pulled his gaze away and lurched to his feet, mumbling something about checking on the girls as he stumbled down the steps to the backyard. He heard Myles chuckle but ignored the man.

He stood at the bottom of the rope ladder. "How are you girls doing?"

"We're fine. Go away." Beatrice offered her usual charming side.

Peyton giggled. "No boys, Seth. Don't you see the sign?"

"Just checking." He looked around the space. An enclosed chicken yard sat nearby with a scruffy gray cat lounging on the slightly slanted roof, while a row of raised garden beds filled most of the open area near the river. One of them was full of green seedlings even this early in June. Someone took their gardening seriously.

Closer to the house, several of the men sat on the grass, tall glasses in hand, near a sandbox where a few toddlers played. Laughter rippled around the group.

Community. Seth had experienced it only with his drinking buddies. When he'd cut those ties after his rededication to Jesus, he'd felt so alone. He hadn't dared hang around for fear he'd be sucked back into that lifestyle. Back to Diana. He'd buckled down to his college classes but hadn't made any real friends. Certainly, no girlfriends.

Now, here was this group willing, at least in theory, to welcome him in, but he didn't actually belong. They were all fathers, whereas his charges were his sisters, not his children. Would he ever have a toddler dumping sand down his legs like little Theodore Roper was doing to Wade?

Ava sauntered toward him, causing that swarm of buzzing bees to return. He pointed at the cat on the chicken coop. "I'm surprised they get along."

She grinned and scratched the cat's chin. "This is Taz. He actually lives next door, but he loves hanging out with the chickens. It drove Violet crazy for the longest time, but she finally gave up the fight."

"I heard that!" yelled the girl from above them. "I still

think Sebastian should keep his cat home, but Dad says cats will climb over any fence, and it's not worth fussing about."

Ava angled her gaze up into the leaves. "And besides, you kind of like Taz, I bet."

"He's okay for a cat."

"I love cats!" Peyton peered between the rails. "Seth, can we get a kitten? I'll take care of it, I promise."

"I..."

"They're easier in an apartment than a dog." Ava's eyes glinted in amusement. "You just need a litter box."

He wrinkled his nose. "Yeah, no."

"*Please*, Seth?"

"Do you have a cat?" he asked Ava. "Maybe Peyton could visit yours."

"Alas, I do not, but it's not a bad idea."

"You can have Taz," offered Violet. "Then he won't bother the chickens anymore."

Ava laughed. "You can't give someone else's cat away."

A mutter came from above. "I can try."

There was an awkward silence for a minute, then Seth indicated the garden beds. "Does this whole community take gardening seriously? Everywhere I look, it seems someone is growing something."

She seemed to take his hint, strolling closer to the beds with him... and away from listening ears. "It's partly the community's Italian roots, I think. My great-grandparents were among the first arrivals, helping build the railroad when it came through. Of course, everyone grew their own food back then. My family settled in this pocket valley and kept on gardening, and I guess it rubbed off on new neighbors as they bought land and built houses, too."

"It's kind of cool. It's an area easy to miss since most

people just shoot across the bridge and land up blocks away. I hadn't really been down here before looking for an apartment." Except for the wedding reception. "I didn't know it was a real old-fashioned community."

She nodded and crouched to pluck a weed or two. At least, that's what he assumed she was doing. The sprouts were no more than an inch or so tall, and he wouldn't have known if they were vegetables or not.

Then she straightened and glanced toward the treehouse before leaning closer. "I've got a question for you."

She smelled of gardenias, and he shifted in. "Hmm?"

"Rebekah and Adriana asked if I had room in my Thursday afternoon dance class for a couple of more kids, and I do."

"But I—"

"If you're going to say you can't afford it, they each want to pay for one of your sisters."

Seth pulled back. "I'm not a charity case." Not yet. Not ever, if he could help it.

"Neighborhood, remember? Around here, people chip in and help each other out. You'll have a chance to repay them in some other way, sooner or later." She chewed her lip for a second. "The thing is, I'd been hoping for sixteen kids for the program I wanted to put on, but only fourteen kids are currently registered. So, you'd be doing me a favor, too."

Was it real? Did it make a difference? He studied her until she looked up at him. "How's that?"

"Four groups of four can meld into two groups of eight or eight groups of two. Fourteen isn't divisible by anything."

He felt himself softening. "It's divisible by seven and two. Teacher."

Ava's chin came up. "Your point is?"

That was a grin she was trying to hide, wasn't it? "Just saying."

"Now that we've proved you're brilliant as well as literal, what do you say? It'll be good for them. Violet and Mandy will be there, plus Sabrina Ramirez and Tieri Amato and a slew of other kids they'll be going to school with."

"Any boys?"

"A few. Sebastian from next door. Three others."

"The boy with the escapee cat."

"The very one." Ava smiled.

Seth poked his toe at the garden box. "I really hate being beholden to anyone. This is all too much already. Dixie and Adriana and Rebekah pretending I'm doing them a favor by *allowing* the girls to spend the day with their kids."

"And now me. I get it. Except I'm not pretending, and I don't think they are, either."

"But... why?"

She seemed to be giving his question the serious consideration it deserved. "I guess it's partly because that's just what we do in Bridgeview. But also, I think it's how Jesus wants us to live. You talked about choosing joy the other day." Lightly, Ava traced her fingertips along his tattoo. "About embracing life. So why not embrace the values of this community?"

Seth froze, unable to move. Unable to think as he stared at her tapered fingers shooting tingles down his arm. "Way to throw my words back in my face." Amazing he could get any words out at all.

"That wasn't my intention." Her voice was soft.

"No?" He waited until she looked up and met his gaze.

Go for it? He wasn't that awkward young teen anymore, but he also wasn't proud of the way he'd treated women most of his adult life. Ava was different. Special. Untouched.

"I'm all kinds of crazy for even thinking this, but... would you be interested in going out with me sometime? I don't even know when or how or what to do with my sisters." He took a deep breath. "Sorry. I shouldn't have asked. I'm in no position to—"

"Seth?" Her fingers slid over his arm again. "One condition."

"Oh. Never mind." He stepped backward, and a cat squealed.

Ava reached down and picked up the scruffy cat, who began purring roughly like an engine with one spark plug misfiring. "You're supposed to ask what the condition is."

All he knew is his arm felt cold without her gentle touch. He'd do pretty much anything she said at the moment. "What's the condition?"

She grinned at him. "The condition is that you let Beatrice and Peyton come to dance class every week from now until Labor Day. And that you don't worry about who paid for it."

"That's two conditions."

"Mr. Logical is out again, I see."

"Does that mean I can't collect until I've fulfilled your conditions?" He placed an emphasis on the plural. "Because that's three months. Much too far away."

"I think we could arrange something in the interim. A show of good faith, maybe."

She was not only beautiful; she was smart and funny. He liked her. A lot.

Too much for his own good.

10

*Y*ou missed a great meal at Myles and Adriana's."

At least Brittany was home. By herself. Making pumpkin cranberry muffins, even though it was June. Some people had no respect for seasonal foods.

Britt shot her a fleeting smile. "Mom had already invited me over."

"I know." Ava dipped her finger in the batter and licked it.

"Get out of the bowl."

"It's good stuff. Even though it's not November."

Brittany rolled her eyes. "Who all was there today? I know Adriana loves to cook for a crowd."

"She does. Rebekah and Wade were there, and Dixie and Dan. And Seth and his sisters and have you noticed how much little Jamie is talking? He's pretty smart for not quite two."

"Seth, huh?" Her cousin pressed both hands to the countertop.

"His sisters are really cute. They said—"

"About Seth."

Ava wanted to clutch her feelings close for now. They were too fragile to share. "What about him?" She reached for another dollop of muffin batter.

Britt rapped the back of her hand with her wooden spoon. "Stop deflecting. Is Adriana matchmaking?"

"Everyone in Bridgeview does that if they think they can get away with it. You know how it is."

"Evasive much?"

Ava sighed. "I don't know if she was matchmaking. She invited you, too, you know."

"I'm dating Duncan."

As if there were any chance Ava had forgotten. "Adriana might not know that."

"What, you didn't tell everyone?"

"Don't get snippy with me, cuz. I don't gossip. There's no jealousy involved."

"Sure."

"For reals. I don't love that you're dating him, but that's because I know you're too good for him. If I didn't know it before I walked in on—"

"Stop."

"Hey, you asked."

"I'm a grownup, Ava Elizabeth Santoro."

Yeah, and so was Ava, even if she didn't always feel like it. Did having a serious boyfriend or a wedding ring make the difference? Would that be when she no longer felt like she should sit at the kids' table at Nonna's? Although being a bridesmaid was definitely not the kids' table.

She certainly didn't feel like a child when Seth looked at

her. Just his searing gaze was enough to melt her insides a little in a way Duncan had never done, nor the half dozen casual boyfriends before him. Duncan definitely melted something in Brittany, though. Her resolve, if nothing else.

Ava backed away from the peninsula. "I need to grab my laptop and redo some of my choreography for the Thursday class. It's full now."

"I thought Violet and Mandy were already signed up."

"Um, yeah. Now Beatrice and Peyton are, too. Brings the group to a nicely rounded sixteen."

"Squared."

Brittany was about as annoying as Seth with the literalism.

"Whatever. I can put in the ideas I originally had for the group to evolve and spin."

"Beatrice and Peyton...?"

Drat, Ava had forgotten what Britt knew and didn't know. "Seth's little sisters he has custody of." Might as well get it all over with at once. "They live downstairs from us in 202."

"Oh, isn't that convenient?"

"It's not like that."

"You don't even know him." Brittany waved the wooden spoon at Ava. "He could be a serial killer, for all you know."

Ava laughed. "Nice try, Britt. You know what dating is for? To get to know someone."

Her cousin narrowed her gaze. "Dating? Since when?"

"Since next week, so you haven't missed anything." Yet. She and Brittany had once compared all the details of a date at the end of it, but Ava had lost any interest she'd had in her cousin's love life when Duncan switched gears. Hopefully Brittany would be just as uninterested in Seth. A girl could hope.

"Where are you guys going?"

"Undecided. He has to figure out what to do with his sisters."

Brittany held up both hands, the wooden spoon along with them. "Don't look at me. I don't babysit for anyone."

"I wasn't asking you to."

"Besides, do you really want to take on someone else's kids if you marry him?"

"It's one date, Britt."

"You always told me not to go out with a guy if I didn't think he was husband material."

Caught again. "That should leave Duncan off the table." Off the sofa. Out of Brittany's life and thus forever out of Ava's.

"Ha-ha. Very funny."

"Grabbing my computer now."

Brittany shrugged and began to dollop batter in muffin tins. "Whatevs."

Ava brought her laptop out to the big comfy chair in the living room and plugged in her headphones. She'd play the music over and over while tweaking the choreography. Maybe she'd run it by Dixie later, since her friend had become nearly as invested as Ava in her classes.

And something was up with Brittany. All the proof Ava needed was the baking binge. Hopefully Britt would talk when she was ready.

She watched the avatars sweep gracefully across the screen, but all she could think of was dancing in Seth's arms at Alex and Marley's wedding.

Could there really be a future with him? Brittany was

right about his sisters. Ava had never envisioned herself a stepmom to kids nearly in their teens. But Seth hadn't envisioned being their caregiver, either, and he'd stepped right up to the plate. He'd had a choice, though maybe it hadn't felt like it. She had the choice to step away right now, before she got too involved.

Instead, she'd been reeled in by those deep magnetic eyes. Would Seth be worth the extra responsibilities and issues?

Only time would tell.

༄

"THANKS FOR SEEING ME." Seth watched as his sisters bounced a basketball with Ava's older brother, Peter. Peyton was in her element, and Beatrice looked mildly interested. But the man had offered to teach them how to shoot baskets so his wife, a family law attorney, could talk to Seth without the girls listening in.

"No problem. Dan told me a bit about your situation. First, please let me offer condolences on the loss of your parents. I'm sure that was a shock."

"My dad and stepmother. Yes. My own mom passed away years ago."

"Right. Dan did mention the girls were your half-sisters."

Seth stretched his legs under the picnic table. "Will that make a difference?"

"Is there anyone else who's likely to challenge you for custody? A grandparent or aunt or close family friend? Anyone that comes to mind?"

"My stepmother's sister said something at the funeral,

but I haven't heard from her since." He took a deep breath. "I haven't wanted to contact her to find out if she was serious in case she's been biding her time, and I reminded her."

Sadie nodded. "That's understandable. Was she close to the girls' mom?"

"I don't know for sure. She and her husband live in Pasco. I know the sisters got together for special occasions, but I don't really know her myself. I—" Seth took a deep breath. "I wasn't around much in those years."

"She's stable?"

He could feel his gut sinking. "Her husband's a dentist, and they have no children of their own." Maybe they would be better off with Eliza and John. Maybe Seth was being selfish trying to keep them. It wasn't like he'd been able to keep them in the home they'd grown up in or the school they'd attended. He wasn't offering continuity. Why did he feel so strongly that he was the right choice? Was it only guilt?

"There are a few things the courts look at, should it come to that. The claimant needs to prove he or she can provide for the children financially, emotionally, and mentally. That includes the entire gamut of food, clothing, housing, education, medical care, and stability."

With every word, Seth's hopes fizzled further. "I might as well give up right now. Eliza and John have all that. I don't. I haven't finished college, we're in a two-bedroom apartment, and everything is up in the air."

Sadie regarded him steadily. "Do you think they'd be better off with their aunt?"

"In some ways. But I want them. I want a chance to

make up for their early years when I ignored them. I want to raise them in a community like Bridgeview and make sure they know Jesus. Their aunt won't do that."

"Okay. So, you want to stay in the game."

Peyton threw the basketball and rammed Peter straight in the gut. The guy doubled over as though in pain, staggered a couple of times, then turned and flicked the ball through the hoop. Beatrice caught it and tried for a basket herself. Peter stopped and gave her a few pointers until she landed one.

The look of glee on her face pierced Seth. "Yeah. I want to fight for them."

"I'll represent you. But you need to do your part to get as many of those areas put together as you can."

"Will the girls' desires matter to a judge?"

"They're eight and ten? The judge will certainly consider their opinion, but they're not really old enough for that to hold all the weight we might wish for. One other question. Are you dating someone? Engaged, maybe?"

Ava's face flashed through his mind. "Would that be a good thing or a bad thing?"

Sadie chuckled. "It depends. If you're dating and break up, that shows instability. On the verge of marriage any day now? That will show stability. So, it could go either way."

What would Ava say if he asked her to marry him to lock in custody? She'd do what any sane woman would. Dunk his head in ice water and then run for the hills.

Seth shook his head. "No imminent engagement. No wedding plans. Just a guy who needs one more year of college to get his degree in engineering, but doesn't know when he can take it. A guy who's got a summer job when he really needs something more permanent. On the other hand, Beatrice is excited about learning to cook Chinese with me, so there's that."

"There's a monthly cooking club that meets in the community center." Sadie pointed to the brick building across the street. "It's run by Kass Ferguson. I can email you the info if you're interested. You'd pay month by month, then attend the meeting to help prep up all the meals for the whole club. Then everyone takes home their share."

"That would be pretty awesome, actually. But I bet it costs a lot to get into."

"Oh, I think I saw a half-price coupon the other day. I'll look for it and email it to you if you like."

Half price? That might be affordable then. But was Sadie just another person trying to help out while pretending not to? He eyed her. "Are you a member of this cooking club?"

She shook her head. "Peter did it for a while, since he does most of the cooking at our house and has more flexible hours. But I'm on a sugar-free, carb-cycling diet, so a lot of the meals don't work well for me. Peter decided it was easier to cook from our own menu."

"Sugar-free? I couldn't do that. I'm totally addicted."

"I was, too. I've lost over one hundred pounds in the past couple of years eating this way."

Seth blinked and looked her over. "No way." The woman had curves, but they looked about the right amount to him. Not that he was eyeing another man's wife. "I would never have guessed."

"I look in the mirror and struggle to see what you see. I still see the woman who was nearly three hundred pounds."

"I don't know what to say."

"You don't need to say anything." She smiled at him. "I'm just saying I don't feel sorry for myself not eating sugar or all the junk it hides in. Not everyone has the problem I did, but I'm always happy to tell my story if it will help someone else. All that to say, no, we don't use the cooking club, but it's still a great idea for others."

Laughter came from the basketball court as the two girls ganged up on Peter in an attempt to steal the ball.

"They look pretty well adjusted," Sadie observed.

Seth's heart swelled. "Beatrice isn't usually this happy. I guess she's coming around."

"Any other questions?"

"Not today. I'll be in to officially file my custody claim this week. Maybe Thursday afternoon? The girls will be at dance class then."

"Oh, Ava's group? They'll love that."

"They're pretty stoked." It might even be why Beatrice wasn't trying to disembowel him with her eyes anymore. "And Sadie? Thank you for taking us on. I was so worried about this whole thing." He still kind of was.

She patted his arm. "You're welcome. I try to help out where I can. Email me what you have on the girls' aunt before Thursday if you can. Anything you know."

"Will do."

"Oh, and get on with getting married." She laughed.

Seth tried to find a chuckle of his own.

"Ready, sweetheart?" Peter settled onto the bench beside his wife and pressed a kiss to her cheek.

She gave him such a tender look that Seth was nearly jealous.

Seth surged to his feet. "Hey, Beatrice, want to teach me how to shoot a basket?"

Peyton stood with her hands planted on her hips. "You don't know?"

"Not very well. Would you two give me some pointers?"

Beatrice studied him for a few seconds. "Okay. You have to stand right here."

11

*A*va couldn't stay away. Technically, she was intruding on Seth's work hours, but would Wade care? Not likely, so long as Seth made steady progress on the project. She could help with that enough to make up for the distraction.

He jammed his shovel in the dirt and wiped the sweat off his forehead with his wrist as he watched her cross the street. "Hey."

"Hey, yourself." She grinned and stopped a few feet away, fingering soft needles on the juniper. "Need a hand with anything today? I've got a couple of hours before I need to get ready for work."

Seth glanced toward downtown. "The bistro?"

She nodded. "It's kind of a habit working there, and I need a steady income over the summer."

He quirked a grin. "Dance classes don't earn you the big bucks?"

"If I could run a full slate of them, maybe. I'd need to open my own studio, but that would conflict with my other job." She'd thought teaching would provide the most security, and it did. Sort of. If only the elementary school up the hill would decide yes, they wanted her for the coming academic year. Or maybe she should apply for a regular classroom instead of sticking to music and dance.

Seth studied her for a long moment.

Ava was glad she was dressed for work in old jeans and a navy tank top with her hair tied back in a no-nonsense ponytail, because the way he was looking at her made her blood heat. She angled her head. "What are you thinking?"

He blinked and met her eyes. "It's hard to believe you don't have the world at your fingertips."

She laughed, but it died quickly at the expression on his face. He was serious... but what did he really mean? "Why would I?"

"I've been around the neighborhood enough to know that Santoro means something."

"Not so much in the rest of Spokane, honestly. And, although my parents paid for college and are always willing to be a sounding board, I'm still expected to make my own way through life." Ava plucked a juniper twig and sniffed the coniferous fragrance.

"It was expected of me, too, but I don't think my dad was looking for the path I actually took."

He'd hinted at an unsavory past. Plus, he'd known Dixie when she was at her most volatile. Ava didn't want to think about it too much. What mattered was that he'd changed. That he was redeemed. Forgiven.

"But that's all behind you, right?" It wasn't that her expectations had been too high when she'd been looking for Mr. Right. It's that she hadn't been leaving room for God's redeeming power in someone's life. She wasn't *settling* with Seth. Mr. Right didn't have to look like she'd thought.

"Yeah." He searched her face, looking like he'd say more. Then he shook his head. "Is Friday night good for you? Dan said my sisters could hang out at their house while Dixie's at work."

Relief and excitement bubbled through Ava. Seth wasn't reneging on the date. He really wanted to go out with her. "Friday's great. Where are we going? So I know how to dress."

His gaze took in her faded work clothes. "You're gorgeous no matter what you wear."

She held back a sigh. "Thanks. But lots of restaurants would give me a side-eye at least if I came in wearing this."

"I was thinking of a picnic. I know it's not fancy..." His voice drifted away.

"That sounds perfect. Really."

"You sure?" He stepped closer, like he was going to take her hands in his, but he didn't.

"Yes. It will be more casual, and we can just talk. Get to know each other." She reached for him before realizing he was wearing leather gloves.

He looked her in the eye as he pulled them off and dropped them to the ground.

Ava's heart pounded like it wanted to explode out of her chest at his intense gaze. Then his warm hands caught her waist, tugging her closer until she nestled against his chest, just like during the slow dance they'd shared at her cousin's wedding reception.

He began to dance, right there in the food forest, to music only he could hear, except she almost could, too. His steps were clear and measured as he led her through familiar movements that needed no audible guide.

Seth dipped her and paused, looking down at her. Time stood still for a full measure before he righted her again and twirled her in.

This time when the dance finished, they stayed looking into each other's eyes from only a couple of inches away. There was no audience, not like at the reception. There also wasn't privacy since anyone could drive by or look out a window.

Ava didn't care. She stretched the small space between them and brushed his lips with hers before stepping back, right out of his arms. She probably shouldn't have done that, but she wasn't going to apologize.

"I'm looking forward to Friday." Seth's voice sounded a little raspy.

"Me, too."

"But now... I guess I should get to work here."

Still their eyes seemed locked together, just like Ava wished their lips were. But he was right. He was on the clock, and she shouldn't be distracting him. "Do you, uh, need a hand today? Or would you get more done without me here?"

His smile softened. "You're definitely a distraction, but you're welcome to stay."

SETH STOOD in the doorway of the church's multi-purpose room, watching Ava as she worked with the sixteen kids. They looked to be a wide range of ages, from maybe six or so to Violet and Beatrice. The kids were good. Most of them had obviously been doing this a while, but his attention kept returning to Ava.

To think he'd thought her a klutz the first time he'd met her. Perhaps she wasn't to blame for nearly bowling him over, but no one had bumped her elbow and caused her to spill the wine glass. He knew. He'd been watching her... as she'd been watching him.

She was lithe and beautiful and patient with the kids, moving between them, correcting them gently, showing them again the correct forms when they faltered. Then she called them together and led them through a series of stretches in a cool-down sequence.

Seth watched Beatrice struggle with the stretch where she sat next to Violet, who was ignoring her as she whispered to the girl on the other side. Peyton, however, seemed to be created of more ligament than bone, able to bend practically anywhere.

He breathed a prayer that this class would be good for both girls, that Beatrice would find her place in the neighborhood. The registered letter that had been in his pocket still weighed heavily, though he'd left it with Sadie along with other paperwork just fifteen minutes back.

Eliza was filing for custody. If only he knew which was best for the girls. He'd need to broach the topic to them carefully. Sensitively.

It would be much easier to pursue Ava if he didn't have his sisters. He'd finish his degree in spring and be able to offer her something besides being a broke guy with too many responsibilities.

Seth stilled. It was way too soon to be thinking of that kind of permanence, true. But there were paths, and the one he and Ava might possibly be on could lead to...

marriage. The one he and his sisters were on didn't seem to mesh. How could he ask a gorgeous woman like Ava to take on two kids that belonged to neither of them?

Yet his sisters belonged *with* him. Did he simply feel a need to make up for the way he'd abandoned his family and served only himself for so long? Maybe? It was impossible to untangle all the strands.

The kids slapped Ava's palm as they scurried past her, class over. His sisters were in that noisy group, but when Ava met his gaze overtop of all their heads, the world stood still, containing only the two of them and the strangest buzzing sensation of his life.

He was a goner, plain and simple.

Tomorrow he would kiss her. Not that sweet whispery brush she'd bestowed on him a couple of days ago in the food forest, but something more. Much more, like a man kisses a woman he is passionately in love with.

Too soon, Donahue. Much, much too early.

But was it? Oh, he'd need to hold back. Be careful not to ruin everything. He was a new creation in Christ, and Ava was pure and sweet. Everything Diana hadn't been. Not that his actions had been exemplary.

Why did he keep thinking of Diana? She was his past, part of the murky years when he'd been running from God. He likely owed her an apology at some point in time. Dixie kept in touch with a few of the old crowd. She was stronger than Seth, that was for sure, but she might know how to find Diana.

And then Ava stood near enough he could smell her fragrance as she chatted with one parent then another as they came to pick up their children.

Peyton, eyes shining, grabbed Seth's hand and bounced

beside him until he thought his arm would be pulled from its socket. "That was so fun! Thank you for making all my dreams come true."

Beatrice muttered something beneath her breath.

Seth followed her gaze to where Violet and the other girl went out the door, arms wrapped around each other and heads bent close together. See, this was why he wasn't equipped to deal with preteens, especially girls. What could he do about Violet? Nothing. He could only hope this wouldn't ruin the day every week when Adriana and Myles had offered to keep his sisters, but if Beatrice and Violet were at odds, Beatrice would only be more miserable.

Lord? Help!

"Okay, girls, let's go."

Peyton dashed over to Ava and squeezed her around the middle. "Thank you, Ms. Ava! I just love to dance." She beamed up with the sunniest expression in the world.

Ava rubbed Peyton's shoulder and smiled down at her. "I'm so glad you and Beatrice were here today. It was fun having you both. Thanks for coming, Beatrice."

She was amazing. So good with the girls. Of course, she was. She was a teacher. All the kids probably loved her. If Beatrice didn't yet, she would.

"See you tomorrow?" he asked Ava softly.

"You couldn't keep me away." Her blue eyes caught his.

"In the morning? But tomorrow at five, too?"

"For sure. To both."

"Seth!" yelled Peyton.

"Duty calls." Seth squelched his reluctance to leave Ava behind, but she no doubt had things to tidy up in the studio. She had a life beyond him and the girls, while he was quickly forgetting he had the same. Finally, he turned away and caught up to his sisters. "Hey. Glad you had fun."

Beatrice shrugged, but Peyton chattered enough for them both as they crossed the parking lot and took the shortcut to the western end of Bridgeview where they lived.

Finally, she paused for air just long enough for Seth to get a word in edgewise. "Question for you two."

Beatrice looked up at him with her eyebrows raised.

"How well do you two know your Aunt Eliza? What do you think of her?"

"Aunt Eliza is amazing!" Peyton proclaimed, swinging Seth's arm.

Beatrice harrumphed. "She's okay, but I don't like Uncle John."

Was it Beatrice's sour attitude, or was there more to it? "What about him don't you like?"

"He thinks we're little kids who want to sit on his lap."

Alarm bells rang. "Does that make you uncomfortable?"

Beatrice shrugged while Peyton said, "Not me! I like hugs."

Seth managed to keep his tone light as he changed the subject. "What do you think of making sesame chicken tonight?"

"Do we have to eat veggies?" wheedled Peyton.

"Yup. There's broccoli in the recipe." A few times this week, a bag of fresh garden produce had been waiting by the apartment door when he arrived home at the end of the day. Whoever his secret benefactor was, he was grateful. Feeding these girls wasn't cheap.

She made a grimace of disappointment then scampered ahead to the playground to zip down the slide a few times while he and Beatrice walked more slowly. A few teen boys played three-on-three at the basketball court as they approached. It seemed pretty rare that no one was using the common area beneath the bridge.

The boys called hello as they passed, and Peyton rejoined him.

Seth let a relieved sigh escape. This was a good neighborhood. A safe place for his sisters. But he needed to figure out if there was anything to Beatrice's issues with her uncle. Because Seth would fight triply hard to gain permanent custody if there was even a smidge of doubt about the kind of household the girls would go to.

12

*A*va smoothed her lacy top over her khaki capris then turned her attention to her hair. She gathered it and twisted it into a knot then frowned. Too formal? Should she leave it down? Normally she'd ask Brittany's opinion, but these days, their conversations were limited to more basic topics, like "what's for dinner?" and, "when will you be home?"

Britt lounged in Ava's doorway, though. "I can't believe you're going out with a guy who's taking care of two kids. Who wants an insta-family? Not me."

It hadn't been Ava's first choice, either. "I think it's sweet that he'll fight for his sisters. It's not like they're his kids, and even if they were, a guy can change."

Her cousin laughed. "Says the girl who's been looking for Mr. Perfect all her life."

Sure beat settling for a jerk like Duncan. "Nothing wrong with aspiring to the best God has for me."

"Yeah. Sure."

Ava looked at her cousin in the mirror, but Britt didn't meet her gaze. "You okay?"

"Me? Yup. Everything's dandy." But the glance was too quick then gone.

"You can talk to me. You know that."

"Funny girl. I guess I should get changed, too. Duncan's coming at five-thirty."

Ava kept her voice light. "Where are you guys going tonight?"

"Not sure." More with the evasive answers and the evasive looks. How much should Ava push?

Brittany wandered away, and Ava pinned her twist in place. She could always let her hair down later if she wanted. Then she touched up her makeup before returning to the living room. Brittany paged through a cookbook. Hadn't she said she was changing? But she'd have another half hour after Ava left with Seth. Plenty of time.

The doorbell rang before she could decide whether to push her cousin or not. A glance into the peephole confirmed it was Seth. "See you later, Britt. Not sure when I'll be home, but I might be early." Why she said that, she didn't know. Maybe a warning?

Then she opened the door to see Seth with a bundle of wildflowers in his hand.

"I know these aren't fancy..." he began.

"They're perfect." She smiled at him and reached for an antique mason jar Nonna had given her. They'd go perfect together. "Seth, I'd like you to meet my cousin and room-mate, Brittany. Britt, this is Seth."

Britt glanced up. "Hi, Seth."

"Nice to meet you." But Seth's gaze was fixed on Ava

when she turned from arranging the colorful stalks. He held out his hand. "Shall we?"

She nestled her hand into his with a feeling of coming home, even though she was leaving. "See you in a while, Britt."

No answer, but the door clicked shut, and she and Seth headed down the two flights of stairs to the building's front door hand-in-hand. He handed her into an older model car, clean as a whistle. "Manito Park okay?"

"Sounds lovely."

He grinned at her as he wiped his hands on his jeans. "Sorry. I'm nervous."

"Don't be." But she was one to talk. She could barely keep breathing in his presence, especially when he smiled at her like that.

He drove past the bistro then jigged and jogged southeast toward Manito. Ava studied his profile while pretending not to. He glanced over. "Do I have dirt on my face?"

"I'd have to look closer. But, you know, I've seen you with dirt on your face."

"And it didn't send you running?"

His voice was serious enough that she knew he wasn't just talking about the obvious. He had a past. Her gaze landed on the tattoo on his arm. It had been partially intended to cover something else, he'd told her, but what? The lines were a little thicker in some parts than others, but that could just as easily be the design. She touched the tattoo. "Should I be running?"

"I hope you don't, but I wouldn't blame you if you did." He took a deep breath and laid his hand palm up on the console between them.

She slipped her hand into his and lightly twined their fingers. "What's got you worried?" Because this wasn't like him.

"I don't know what to do," he started then fell silent.

Ava waited.

"The girls' mom's sister has put in a bid for custody. Would that be best for them?"

"Do you have an attorney? Because my sister-in-law—"

"Sadie. Dan got me in touch with her."

"Okay. Good. She's an expert in family law."

"She seems competent. Like she'll do whatever is best for the girls."

Ava nodded. "Do you think their aunt would be the best choice?" Because she liked the girls just fine, but Seth on his own would be a much more attractive catch. Did that thought make Ava a selfish person? Balancing the two sides was hard.

"In some ways. She's married to a dentist. So, they're solid. Except for two things. I'm not sure they're Christians, and her husband makes Beatrice uncomfortable."

"Oh. You might want to get her into counseling to figure that out."

He slid his hand away to turn a corner. "I agree with you, but that's more expense. Which only reminds me how much better off they'd be in a dentist's household than with a guy who doesn't have an education and doesn't have a permanent job."

"Rebekah would be happy to talk to her. She counsels at the elementary school. Plus, don't the girls spend some time with her and the kids during the week?"

"I hate taking advantage of people."

"I get that. I do. But just a few words to her and she can be watching for a chance to steer the conversation over that direction." How much should she say? "Rebekah has a history of sexual abuse. She'd definitely know red flags to look for."

"Maybe." Seth tapped his signal light for the parking lot. "This is one of my favorite places in the city. Let's not worry about the girls anymore tonight. There will be plenty of time for that later."

"Deal." But it was a definite reminder that she couldn't ever expect his complete attention. Part of him would always be looking out for his sisters... unless they moved to live with their aunt. But he'd still be worrying if he didn't trust the woman's husband.

Lord, do I really want to keep seeing this man?

Too bad the answer was always yes. Seth was worth it.

⁘

"Want to eat right away or go for a wander and come back to get the picnic later?" Seth turned off the ignition.

"Let's come back in a bit." Her eyes gleamed with excitement. Was it the park, the picnic, or... did he dare think it might be for him?

"Stay put. I'm coming around for you."

She grinned and bounced a little on the seat, making him laugh as he rounded the hood. She reminded him a bit of Peyton. No wonder his youngest sister adored Ms. Ava. Seth kind of did, himself.

Then she slid out of the car and into his arms. It was everything Seth could do to take a step back and hold both her hands rather than go straight to the kissing like he wanted. No rushing. Life was too uncertain to get entangled too quickly.

He'd kept away from women since Diana, keeping busy with college and then his sisters, so it wasn't just that he didn't trust himself. But there was definitely that aspect, too. He hadn't tested himself since he'd come back to the Lord. Not with a woman he respected... but shouldn't he have respected Diana and the others, too?

Enough. He was here to have a good time. To get to know Ava. To look into the future, not the past. "Which is your favorite part of the park?"

"I love Rose Hill." She tugged him toward the stone wall surrounding it.

He fell into step beside her. "Really? I'm surprised. I didn't expect a formal garden. I thought you'd go for something more free-flowing, like the Ferris Garden with all the perennials."

Ava swung their hands between them. "Ah, but I love choreography and order. Everything should be right where it belongs at the right moment in time. What's your favorite?"

Interesting. "Hmm. That's hard. A couple of weeks ago it was the lilac area when it was all in bloom. Now maybe it's the Japanese garden since some of the trees are still in blossom. Or Mirror Pond. I like water."

She giggled. "Good thing, since you got soaked yesterday when the water line leaked."

Seth nudged her with his shoulder. "And you laughed at me. I couldn't believe it. So hardhearted."

"Not at all." Ava broke into a run, dragging him behind her.

What was that supposed to mean? His emotions

hiccupped. Her heart was soft, not hard. And, boy, did he know it. Seth stopped on the path. When she glanced back to see why, he gave a little tug and spun her into his arms. Dating a dancer was fun.

But his heart stuttered when he looked into Ava's blue eyes just inches from his. "I take that back," he whispered.

Her gaze dipped to his lips then back up. "Take what back?" Her voice was just as low as his.

Seth's hands caressed her back then wrapped around her waist snugly. "There's nothing hard about you." But that didn't mean she was easy, either. "You're all feminine. All beautiful. All caring."

"You think?"

Did she not see it? Or did she just want more? He could give more. "You're the most amazing woman I've ever met. And I want to kiss you."

Ava tipped her head to one side, her lips lifting just a touch on the corners. "You like kissing amazing women?"

"Only ones I really care about."

"Interesting. I only kiss men I think I'm falling for."

He tried to read her eyes. "Does it happen often?"

"Falling? Very rarely."

Of course, she'd had boyfriends before. It was way too much to expect that she'd reached her mid-twenties without a serious relationship or two. But he came to her with much more baggage than that. Did she guess? He should tell her.

Ava's fingers tangled in his hair, and he tightened his hold around her, closing his eyes and reveling in the feel of her body pressed against his. He'd tell her later. It wasn't fair that she didn't know.

But for the life of him, he couldn't break the spell of this perfect moment and dump his dirty laundry out in front of her right now. She might run, and he couldn't blame her if she did. So he did the only thing he could think of.

Seth cupped the back of her head and kissed her.

He'd meant for it to be smooth and light. Truly.

But when Ava's lips parted for his and her hands roved his head, his neck, his shoulders, he responded to her unspoken request and deepened the kiss. He could lose himself here.

Seth managed — somehow — to keep himself grounded even as his mouth explored hers.

Maybe his old self didn't matter. He was redeemed by Jesus. A new creation. Besides, Ava knew he'd had some wandering years. If she thought about it at all — and he was sure she must have or would at some point — she'd figure out he was far from pure.

New creation.

He needed to remember. With a sigh he broke the kiss and tucked her head into the crook of his shoulder. "What you do to me, woman," he said huskily.

She took a deep trembling breath against his chest. "I think... maybe... we should go see the rose garden."

"Probably." So she didn't want to talk about the kiss? Maybe their lips had already said everything there was to say. He could wait. He could pray that he'd know if he needed to tell her everything about his past or if it had truly been tossed into the deepest sea with a *no fishing* sign. Wasn't that biblical?

Lord, give me wisdom. And control.

13

*S*eth kissed Ava goodnight at her apartment door then made his way down the flight of stairs and let himself into his own place. He set the picnic basket on the counter and emptied the remains into the fridge. They'd barely touched the food. His sisters would be happy to devour it tomorrow.

Oh, Lord.

He sank into the sofa and cradled his face in his hands. Why had Dad and Lori died? Why had Seth thought he was the best one to raise Beatrice and Peyton? He wasn't. Not by a long shot. He should have let Eliza and John take them home right after the funeral. But then he'd never have known Beatrice was uncomfortable with John.

If only Seth were an average Christian guy in his late twenties. One who hadn't rebelled and lost a decade of his life. One who'd finished college, had a decent job, and wasn't fighting for custody of two kids who weren't even his.

How had his life come to this? He really, really didn't want to go down the hill and pick up the girls. Maybe he could call Dan and see if they could stay overnight. But ditching them wasn't fair to them or to Dan and Dixie.

No. Seth was a grownup and needed to act like it. His choices had been set in motion years back, and now he had to live with the consequences. All of them.

But he desperately needed to find some quiet time — soon — to spend in the Word and place his life and future in God's hands *again*. Seek some guidance. Wisdom.

That wasn't tonight. He had responsibilities. Finally, he went out to the car and drove around to the Rantas' house.

An unfamiliar vehicle sat in the driveway, so Seth parked along the street so as not to block the visitor in. He strode up the walk, tapped on the door, and let himself inside.

Tanisha Valdez stood in his line of vision holding a baby.

Now that was a blast from the past. "Hi?" He hadn't known she was expecting, but then he hadn't seen her since he'd cut ties with his old group. Dixie was stronger than he was, still reaching out to everyone.

"Hi, Seth." Tanisha jostled the little one, whose face was red, probably from crying. He rubbed his eyes with a fist.

Poor kid. Tanisha should know better than to keep him out so late. He was obviously out well past his prime.

He met Tanisha's gaze. "Looks like congratulations are in order?"

She raised her eyebrows at him. "More like congratulations to you."

Him? Seth took a step back. What did Tanisha mean? He'd never slept with her. Her child couldn't be his.

Tanisha sighed. "Come into the living room so we can talk."

"I'm here to pick up my sisters. Where are they?"

Dan stepped around the corner, glancing between Seth

and Tanisha. "I put them to bed in Mandy's room a bit ago. They can stay the night. And now I'm heading upstairs. Leave you two to talk."

Seth's brain spun. He was missing something. Something vital. But what? "Okay? Thanks." It would have been nice if Dan had let him know. It would have saved him the trip down the hill and given him a bit of time to think. To regroup after that amazing date with Ava.

But Dan's action had nothing to do with Seth's date, and everything to do with Tanisha and this child.

Lord? Give me wisdom. He traced his tattoo instinctively. *Joy. Life.*

Tanisha shifted the baby in her arms and pointed to the living room seating with her chin. "Have a seat, Seth."

He obeyed, clenching his hands over the armrests. "What's going on? Whose kid is he?"

She met his gaze steadily. "Diana's. And yours."

No. Way. Seth closed his eyes. Good thing he was sitting down, because he felt himself swaying even so. "You must be mistaken."

"I know it must be quite a shock."

Ya think? He shot her a quick glance but saw only compassion. "Where's Diana?"

"Sh-she passed away about a week ago. A stroke brought on by drugs."

Seth reeled, his head slamming against the back of the chair. Diana. So full of life. She couldn't be gone.

"She asked me to find you if anything ever happened to her. I have everything with me in the car. His pack-and-play, his formula, his diapers. Other stuff."

"Wait. Why? Tell me straight what's going on. It's been a long day." And he'd had the most amazing daydream, only to wake up to... this. Whatever *this* was. He tried not to look at the baby, but that ended when Tanisha plopped him into Seth's lap.

The baby arched his back and screamed.

I feel you, buddy. Seth patted the little guy's back but, apparently, that was of no comfort.

Tanisha dug into the massive purse sitting on another chair, pulled out a sheaf of papers, and set it on the end table beside him. "Here's everything you need."

Seth surged to his feet and held out the soggy-bottomed baby. "No. I don't know what you're talking about. You can't just... do this."

"His mother is dead, and you're his father. He's your responsibility. It took me a few days to find you, or I'd have let you know in time to come to Diana's funeral."

This was... real? "Tanisha?" He could feel the begging in his voice. Feel the weakness.

"Look, I'm sorry to spring this on you, Seth. Truly. But he's yours, even though the birth certificate says *father unknown*. Diana swore to me she hadn't been with anyone but you for months. She didn't want to drag you into it all, but that was before she died... and it doesn't change the facts."

Seth couldn't hold the baby out at arm's length any longer. The kid must weigh twenty pounds at least. *His* kid? He licked his lips and looked down at the dark eyes staring back at him beneath blond wisps. "What's his name?"

"Leo."

"Tanisha, I can't do this." He sank back into his chair and set the baby on the floor.

"Dan told me you'd taken on your half-sisters after their parents died."

Seth nodded.

"So, I'd say you've got the heart to take in another stray that shares your DNA."

"I don't have a degree. I don't have a permanent job. I don't have anything to give anyone." What had he been thinking, asking Ava out? Kissing her like his life depended on it? He wasn't good enough for her. Not even close.

The evidence plucked at Seth's leg hairs right this second. And it hurt.

"If you want to put him into foster care, that's up to you. Your choice." Tanisha dug in her purse some more and came out with a pacifier. "Here, Leo."

The baby grabbed it and jammed it in his mouth.

"I think that's everything. I saw you'd driven down, which is convenient. I'll just transfer Leo's things over and be on my way."

"You can't..."

Tanisha ignored his halfhearted words. She swung the purse over her shoulder and scurried out the front door. Over the next couple of minutes, he heard several vehicle doors slam, then a car drove away.

Leaving him with a baby.

Seth looked up to see Dan taking a seat nearby. "I'm sorry," his friend said simply.

Not half as sorry as Seth was. This baby was his? And he was now responsible in the blink of an eye?

"Know how to change a diaper?"

Seth shook his head. "It's never come up."

"Let me show you. And if you want to spend the night here yourself, you and Leo, you're welcome. The sofa is reasonably comfortable. I've spent a night or two there myself, back in the day. Just so you know, Dixie will be home from her shift at Antonio's in about half an hour, though, and Henry wakes up at the crack of dawn."

Tempting, but no. "I'll take him home. But I'm going to need a lot of help. I can't even comprehend how much."

"Let's start with that diaper."

AVA DIDN'T KNOW what time Brittany had come home, but thankfully her bedroom door was shut and her handbag was on the shelf when Ava wandered into the kitchen the next morning, twisting her hair into a knot.

She'd spent much too long staring at the ceiling last night, wide awake, reliving every moment of her date with Seth yesterday. The kisses near Rose Hill, the kisses in the butterfly garden, the kisses in the conservatory, the kisses in the Japanese garden. They'd barely touched the picnic, though Ava was sure it would have been delicious.

Now, she was famished. Was it too early to text Seth and thank him for the amazing time she'd had? Surely his sisters woke up before nine, but he might be busy getting them breakfast or something like that.

Ava hugged herself. She could be patient.

It had been easy for her to forget his responsibilities yesterday, just as it was the mornings she gave him a hand at the food forest, since his sisters were rarely around. But she was head over heels in love with Seth, and she could handle Beatrice and Peyton in their life so long as she got moments like yesterday alone with Seth.

She flipped on the coffee pot and wandered across the space to the window overlooking the river a few blocks down the hill. When the brew beeped its completion, she poured a cup, doctored it, and settled into her cozy chair with her open Bible.

Pastor Tomas had challenged the congregation to read a chapter of Philippians every day in June as he preached through the epistle. Today she was on chapter four... again.

Not for the first time, Ava wondered about Euodia and Syntyche. What troubled the relationship of two women commended for working beside Paul for the gospel?

The command to rejoice in everything was for those two as well as the rest of the Philippian church. As well as for Ava and other believers today. Let gentleness be evident. Check. Don't be anxious but give every situation to God with thanksgiving. *Thank You for Seth.* Check.

And then the peace of God would guard her heart and mind. She didn't need to worry about Seth's sisters or his job or why she was falling for the man who didn't seem to be Mr. Perfectly Right... but paradoxically, did seem to be.

Finally, brothers and sisters, whatever is true, whatever is noble, whatever is right, whatever is pure, whatever is lovely, whatever is admirable — if anything is excellent or praiseworthy — think about such things.

And then, there it was again. *And the God of peace will be with you.*

Ava closed her eyes and thought through the list as her heart lifted. In the distance, she heard a baby wail, but she quickly pulled her mind back to the scripture. *If anything is excellent or praiseworthy...*

Thank You, Jesus. I just want to fill myself and my life with things that honor You. Things that bring You joy will bring me joy. Lord, I want that to be Seth — You know what's in my heart — but I pray that You will guide us both. I know he's seeking Your will, too, even though he hasn't been practicing that all his life. He is now, so please bless him in it.

"Hey." Britt crossed the space into the kitchen wearing a baggy T-shirt and workout shorts, her long, messy hair strewn across her shoulders.

"Hi." Ava could only be thankful she'd had a few minutes with the Lord before her cousin wandered in. She needed the grounding. "Sleep okay?"

Her back to Ava, Brittany shrugged then poured a coffee. "I kept waking up. Kept hearing a baby cry, but there isn't anyone in the building with a baby, is there?"

Ava shook her head. "Not that I know of." She frowned. "I thought I heard one a few minutes ago. Maybe one of our neighbors had overnight company."

"Maybe." Britt settled into the sofa and leaned her head back. "Ah... the weekend."

"Did you have a good time last night?" Ava wasn't sure she wanted to know. She also wasn't sure she wanted to share her own news. It felt like something to hold close for a while, first.

Britt took a sip, not meeting Ava's eyes. "Yeah. We went to a club on the North Hill."

Don't ask what kind of club. Don't. But wasn't Ava at least a bit responsible for her cousin since they were roommates and all? "I'm worried about you," she said cautiously.

"Don't be. What are you up to today? I thought I'd bake."

"It's supposed to be over ninety degrees today. I mean, cookies are probably worth it, but—"

"Pies. Muffins. You want cookies, too?"

The third-floor apartment was going to be stifling with

no air-conditioning and limited cross-ventilation from the windows. "Whatever you want to make is fine by me."

"Okay." Britt still didn't meet her gaze.

Something was wrong, but pushing wasn't going to get Ava anywhere. Was it?

14

*S*eth's new best friend was going to be his phone's search function. How else could he figure out what to do with a ten-month-old? What to feed him? How to stop his tears?

This couldn't be happening.

It really couldn't, but the packet Tanisha had left him included some enlightening documents. Birth certificate. A paper stating that Seth Donahue was Leo's father and should raise him in the event of his mother's death. Had Diana expected to die, or was she simply one who covered all her bases when she was sober?

It looked like the latter, because there was a letter addressed to Seth dated nearly a year back, well before Leo's birth. Diana promised she'd stayed clean once she'd known she was pregnant, that she didn't want to damage the baby. That she missed Seth and was looking forward to having a piece of him in her life, even though she knew he was too good for her now, and she didn't want to wreck his future.

Seth scrubbed at his eyes and glanced at the baby strapped into a seat on a kitchen chair a few feet away, smearing Seth's last banana into his wispy hair.

Diana's packet also included information on getting DNA testing so he'd know for sure she was telling the truth.

But how could he doubt her when he remembered the several months they'd lived together? When he looked into one of his baby pictures staring back at him from that high chair?

Getting the test done was likely a good idea, though. Confirmation and all.

How on earth was he going to manage now?

Despair had been swirling through his heart and mind all night, keeping him awake even during Leo's intermittent naps. He'd been at the end of his rope for the past two months, ever since Dad's and Lori's deaths.

But now. How could he reach out of these depths? Joy was like a kite bobbing away, its string broken.

He'd been dreaming yesterday with Ava, believing for a few blissful hours that life was his to embrace. That with her at his side, he could somehow overcome the bad hand he'd been dealt.

Now it looked like he'd dealt the hand himself. He had no one else to blame.

Maybe he should let Eliza and John take the girls. Then he could focus on raising his son.

Leo was his son.

He stared at the baby.

The baby stared back, his lower lip quivering into a pout.

Seth managed a smile, fake as it was.

Leo smiled back, showing four tiny white teeth, then kicked his chubby legs and smacked banana goo onto the plastic tray.

He was cute. Peyton was going to love him. At least, until he woke her up at night. Beatrice would...

Seth couldn't do this. He was a single guy without a decent job. He could not be responsible for three children.

I can do all this through him who gives me strength.

The preacher at Bridgeview Bible had talked about that last week. Seth vaguely remembered the memory verse from his childhood. That was in Philippians somewhere. He should look it up.

Leo's eyes lost focus as his face reddened. He grunted.

Had the baby choked on something?

A putrid stench filled the air. Seth had almost forgotten that not all diapers would be soaked with urine. This... was the other.

He was not cut out to be a parent, especially not by himself. But there was no one else to clean this mess, so it fell to him. He eyed the baby until the grunting stopped and Leo turned a sunny smile his direction again.

Seth needed to check the baby section of a department store downtown and find the gas masks.

∂ ‿ ‿

SETH WASN'T IN CHURCH.

Ava tried to turn her mind from the realization she hadn't heard from him for an entire day. He hadn't seemed to have any hesitation about pursuing her Friday night, but it looked like he'd been attacked by a massive dose of self-doubt since then. Maybe Britt was right. She should call him... or go downstairs and knock on his door.

But now she needed to focus on Pastor Tomas's sermon from Philippians three. *Further, my brothers and sisters, rejoice in the Lord!*

Joy. She needed to cling to that. Seth could not define it for her — only Jesus could. Paul had just written about how Jesus had humbled Himself, identifying as a fully human servant while remaining God, and submitting to a horrific death on the cross to bridge the gap between God and man.

Now that was worthy of celebration. Of deep joy. Was it okay to be a little frustrated, sad — even angry — and still cling to the solace Jesus came to bring? If not, Ava was sunk, because the wrestling match in her heart and mind didn't stop.

In the scripture reading, Paul talked about how he'd been the exemplary Jew, following the law right down to the letter, but now he considered it all a loss, because through all that he'd missed knowing Jesus, the heart of the faith he'd been orbiting. He set aside all his perfect history, simply pressing toward the goal God had called him to.

Sitting in the pew between Dafne and Mom, Ava closed her eyes. She identified with Paul. The *before* Paul. The one who tried to do everything right and... oh man. And who looked down on people who didn't have it all together.

But Paul counted his previous life a loss. A negative.

Join together to follow my example.

What example? The Perfect Paul example? No. The one where he'd set all that aside, his only goal now to be worthy of a citizenship in heaven through Jesus' sacrifice, not because he himself was good enough.

Ava didn't dare fidget in her seat, not with her mother

beside her. She could almost feel the Mom-glare that had helped keep her in line through her childhood years.

She kept her calm smile in place as she, Dafne, and Gavin walked to her parents' house after church. Okay, her little nephew didn't walk anywhere if he could run or jump. At least his presence kept the conversation non-threatening.

Mom was already in a tizzy. "But it is not her week to come to our house!" she exclaimed to Dad, practically tying her skirt in knots.

Ava froze, and Daf ran into her. "Nonna?"

"Yes!" Mom shot a frustrated glare at Dad. "I only have grilled chicken and salad planned. Nothing fancy."

Dad slipped his arm around her shoulder. "It's fine, Betta. Mamma isn't here to judge your cooking."

"Then why?" Mom looked frantically between them all.

Ava took a deep breath. "She probably heard I went on a date Friday and wants the details."

Dafne let out a little giggle.

"You dated?" Mom asked. "Why am I always the last to know?"

"It was one date. Not a big deal." Especially since Seth had pretty much ghosted Ava since. "But who knows what seems a big deal to Nonna?"

Voices sounded on the front steps.

Ava whirled to face her mother. "What can I help you with? Do you need another chicken breast thawed?"

"No, no. I have plenty."

Her mother was a basket case, like she could never do anything right around her mother-in-law. Well, Nonna never hesitated to say it like she saw it. Ava wasn't overly fond of her grandmother's bluntness or nosiness herself. Especially not now, when she suspected it was all for her.

"You've improved so much since your fall!" Sadie gushed. "Look at you, walking all that way from the church."

"Tired, Nonna?" came Peter's voice. "Would you like a seat in the living room?"

"Where are Dino and Betta?"

"Probably in the kitchen," replied Peter.

"Go!" Mom gave Dad a little push.

He shook his head, grinning all the while, as he went toward the living room. "Hello, Mamma. Good to see you looking so well."

"You saw me at church, and you saw me on Friday," came Nonna's irritated voice.

Ava exchanged glances with her sister. Nonna sounded in fine form. "Dafne, you and Gavin go entertain her. I'll help Mom."

"Grilled chicken in more ways than one," grumbled Daf with a grin as she steered her almost-three-year-old past the island.

Days like this Ava wondered how her cousins got along so well with their crotchety grandmother. To hear her speak, Jasmine adored Nonna, and Francesca wasn't far behind. "Put me to work."

"Is it true it's your fault?" Without waiting for an answer, Mom turned to the fridge and pulled out a container of marinating chicken.

All Ava's aunts got along with their mother-in-law, even Winnie, who'd remarried after her husband — Nonna's son — had passed away. Why was Mom so afraid of the old woman?

If Ava married Seth, she wouldn't even have a mother-in-law. Ava stopped cold in the middle of the kitchen. That was a weird thought, and one she definitely shouldn't even be thinking, whether with relief or not. The guy ghosted her, remember? He lived right downstairs but seemed to have vanished.

Of course, she hadn't called him, either, but wasn't she supposed to let the guy do the pursuing? Maybe. Maybe not.

She shoved the thought out of her mind, washed her hands, and began chopping the heads of romaine lettuce her mom had set on the island.

"Ava Elisabetta!"

Her gaze lifted to see her grandmother standing in the doorway. "Hi, Nonna."

"What is this I hear about you?"

She forced a smile. "I guess it depends on what you heard." And the old woman should know better than to heed gossip.

"That you were kissing a man in the butterfly garden at Manito Park."

Mom gasped. "You said it was only a date, but that sounds like more."

"Word gets around." Ava whacked her large knife across the stem end of the lettuce. And why hadn't Nonna got wind of any of Britt's escapades? Oh, because her cousin was smart enough to do it in the privacy of the apartment?

"Who is he?" Mom sounded hurt.

Ava tried to grab onto some of that peace and joy she'd felt in church, but it was long gone. "Seth Donahue. You probably don't know him."

"Then you should invite him to Sunday lunch."

"I should meet him, too," Nonna replied. "I can come again next week."

Ava just bet she could. "I think that would be putting the cart before the horse."

"But if you were *kissing*..." Mom protested.

"Relax." Ava set down the knife and looked between them. Oh, and there were Dad and Dafne in the doorway, Peter and Sadie right behind them. "Seriously. Let me figure out when — or if — to present him to the family. It was one date, people." And yeah, it didn't look respectable that there'd been kissing. Hopefully Nonna's informant hadn't hung around long to watch, or followed them around the park for a while. She pinned a look on her dad. "I think Mom needs you to fire up the grill."

"Of course." Dad squeezed her shoulder on his way past. Peter followed him out the patio door to the deck.

A cell phone rang, and Sadie retreated into the living room. "Hello, Sadie Santoro speaking."

Nonna pivoted, Ava's sins momentarily forgotten as she tried to overhear Sadie's side of the conversation.

Ava would take the reprieve while she had it, because it was sure to be short-lived.

"You're kidding me! Wow, that certainly adds a complication. ... Are you sure? You can't undo that, you know. ... Yes, I can. How about in an hour or so? ... Yes, I can meet you there. ... I'll be praying for you."

"Who was that?" Nonna wasn't the only one eaten alive by curiosity.

Sadie wrapped an arm around Nonna's shoulders and smiled at her. "A client, which means it was confidential."

Nonna scowled. "It's Sunday, not your office hours."

"I sometimes do pro bono work on my own time."

Who could it have been? Not that Ava knew everyone Sadie knew, but the pro bono aspect caught her attention. Was she working with anyone other than Seth?

Maybe Seth was going to let the girls' aunt take them. It might be better for them to live with an established couple than with a single guy who was dating. Well, if he was dating.

Why hadn't he called or texted since Friday night?

His silence ate Ava alive.

"I'll take the meat out now, Betta." Dad pressed a kiss to Mom's cheek and retrieved the container from the fridge.

Sadie followed him out to the deck, where she set her hands on Peter's hips. Peter returned the gesture, looking deeply into Sadie's eyes as they stood there. Probably Sadie was telling him about the phone call. Then he glanced at Ava through the patio door before pulling Sadie close in a hug.

Had he looked at Ava because the call involved her... or because he'd felt her stare?

Enough. Right now, she needed to finish prepping the lettuce. There'd be plenty of time to worry about all this later. For now, she just needed to keep Nonna and Mom off the scent.

15

*T*hat's not as good a playground as ours." Peyton stood beside the car with her arms crossed.

"I thought you'd like a change of scenery." Seth backed out of the car with Leo in his arms. "Beatrice, can you please get the diaper bag?"

"Why, so you don't have to be seen carrying a pink purse?"

"Maybe." What on earth had Diana been thinking? But then guilt swarmed Seth all over again. "But mostly because I only have two hands."

"Moms do it all by themselves, no problem." She reached in and grabbed the bag.

"Hey." He waited until she looked up at him, moisture swimming in her eyes. "I know you miss your mom."

"You don't know anything."

"I'm trying, Bea. I really am."

Peyton dashed up the nearby slide, making it to the top. At least one sister seemed okay.

Seth set the baby on the grass, and the little guy lifted his legs and whimpered. "Not used to the prickles, buddy?"

"Why do you have a stupid baby, anyway?"

"His mother died."

"Everyone's mother dies. Or their dad. Or both."

"Aw, Beatrice. I'm so sorry." There was no point in reminding her that he'd lost as much as she had. She was just a kid, and her hurt was real.

She shrugged and turned away with her arms crossed, but her shoulders shook.

A car, much newer and nicer than his, parked nearby, and Sadie swung out of the driver's seat. She grabbed a briefcase out of her backseat and strode toward them. "Hi, Seth. Hi, Beatrice. So, this is the little guy? What's his name again?"

Beatrice glared at the woman and stalked away.

"This is Leo." Seth watched Beatrice as she joined her sister on the monkey bars. "And Beatrice is having a moment."

"Poor kid. She's gone through so much."

"She has." Seth lowered himself to the ground beside Leo, but where he could still watch the play equipment. "She was observing that everyone in our household" —and wasn't that a bedraggled crew? — "is motherless."

"Me, too."

Seth looked at Sadie in surprise.

"My mother died when I was sixteen, so I was a little older than your sisters. She was my adoptive mom. I met my birth mom for the first time a couple of years ago. All that to say, I have a clue how much upheaval your sisters are going through. And you."

Leo crawled a few inches, but he wouldn't get far if he

kept trying to minimize his contact with the grass. It was almost funny. First time Seth had felt anything akin to a smile since late Friday night.

He looked at Sadie. "I don't know what to do." Now that was an understatement.

"And you're wondering, once again, if you should pass the care of the girls on to their aunt and uncle."

"I hate giving up on them."

Peyton dangled from the monkey bars by her knees while Beatrice dropped to the sand below.

"Sometimes the hardest thing is determining what is best for someone else and then following through."

"Ain't that the truth?" But the humor didn't get past his voice. "It's the knowing I'm struggling with. And the fact that the girls were already stretching me thin before Leo was dropped in my lap." He remembered Tanisha's action. "Literally."

"I'm sure.

"Makes the good old days of caring for two sisters seem pleasant and simple. Can I honestly raise three kids when I can barely keep a roof over my own head? How do I manage childcare for a baby? Should I give *him* up into the system? Should I give the girls up? Should I give them *all* up? Or none of them?"

Even as he voiced his concerns, the vice tightened around his chest. He couldn't handle this. He couldn't. All he wanted was to be a carefree single guy like he'd been a few months ago. He wanted to pursue a relationship with Ava and finish college and get a decent job.

All those things felt like they were slipping away, never to return.

He couldn't ask Ava to take on his baby from another

woman. His sisters were bad enough, but at least they weren't his offspring, weren't reminders of the years he'd walked away from God.

"Should you talk to the girls' aunt? Maybe you'd have a better feel for the situation if you did that. It might all become very clear, one way or the other."

Seth pulled Leo away from the edge of the sand pit. "I've wondered about that. It just feels like the first step to giving up."

"The fate of the entire world does not rest on your shoulders."

"It feels like it does."

"Maybe you could come to an amicable agreement on sharing custody with them."

He stopped and stared at her. "How do you figure that?"

"Maybe the girls could live with you during the school year, but spend their breaks and summers with their aunt and uncle. Or the other way around."

"I... uh..." He scratched his head, managing to get sand in his hair as he did. Leo had it everywhere already. "That never occurred to me."

"You're an all-or-nothing kind of guy," Sadie observed.

"I guess." He took a deep breath and turned Leo toward the widest expanse of grass while he considered Sadie's words. He could see what she meant. "What about him?"

"There are many childless couples who are praying for a baby. You could have a say in his placement."

"Give him up for adoption?" He'd only considered foster care, and that had been a rough thought. "But he's... mine."

"We'll do the DNA to be sure."

"We don't need to. He's mine."

"You've chosen."

"I... I guess?" And yet, choosing the baby meant not choosing Ava. In his heart, he knew he could never ask her to step into his mess. It had been bad enough with the girls. Leo was not only Seth's, but needed a whole other magnitude of care.

Friday evening would have to keep Seth warm for years to come.

"I need a job." The thought of a college diploma slipped away, hand-in-hand with Ava. "Something that pays enough for childcare and... everything." Something beyond a few catering gigs with Hailey at the bistro or the temp job at the food forest. He'd been thankful for both, but they weren't a long-term plan.

"Peter's dad owns a painting business. I can see if he needs another worker."

Sadie's father-in-law was Ava's dad. Seth shook his head. "No. I can't see that."

"Peter's uncle owns Santoro Electrical. Fancy becoming an electrician?"

"I can't work for your family."

She gave him a half-smile as he reined Leo in yet again. "I know people who hire people."

Seth let out a long breath. "I think I need to move right out of Bridgeview."

"Don't give up on your future, Seth."

His gesture took in the three children. "This is my future."

∽⌣⌣

AVA TRUDGED up the wide staircase in the apartment building, eyeing Seth's door on the second-floor landing. Should she march over there and pound on his door? But his car wasn't in the parking lot. He wasn't home. How could he be home when he was avoiding her?

If only she could forget how she felt around him. How safe she'd felt in his arms, how treasured his kisses made her feel.

She let herself into the third-floor apartment she shared with her cousin and stopped dead in the doorway as the fragrance of sweets billowed out on a wave of heat. The table was extended to its full length and was covered in cookies. There must be ten or twelve dozen, and none of them had been created when she left for church.

Brittany piped icing around a triple layer chocolate cake. "Hey."

Ava set her purse on the shelf and kicked off her heeled sandals. "What's going on?"

Her cousin blew a strand of hair from in front of her eyes, though the entire messy ponytail looked about to become undone. She wore the gray tank top and the baggy workout shorts she usually slept in. "I'm baking."

"I see that. What did you do with all the stuff you baked yesterday?"

"Dropped it off at the women's shelter. I did keep back a dozen of the peanut butter chocolate chip cookies you like."

They were Ava's last concern at the moment. "And what are you doing with all this?"

"Maybe the same thing? I don't know."

"Talk to me, Britt."

"And tell you what, Aves?" Her voice was sarcastic but shaky.

"You're my cousin and my best friend. I care about you.

I know you bake when you're stressed out, but I've never seen you let loose like this before."

Brittany shook her head but didn't meet Ava's gaze.

"What did Duncan do?"

Red shot up Brittany's cheeks. "Why do you assume it was him?"

"Um... you're kind of giving it away."

"You just want a chance to say *I told you so*."

Ava's heart sank. "Never, Britt. I love you far too much for that."

"Go ahead. Say it."

"Tell me what happened."

"He hasn't come by since Friday. He hasn't called or texted. Nor has he picked up when I've called him."

Ava sank onto a chair beside the heavily laden table, picked up a cookie, and broke it in half. "He ghosted you."

"You bet your sweet life he did."

"Before or after?"

Brittany glowered at her. "What are you talking about?"

"Did you have sex with him?"

Tears dribbled down Brittany's face. "I wasn't going to..." And then the floodgates opened.

Ava dropped the cookie and wrapped her arms around her cousin. "Oh, Britt. I'm so sorry."

"Not as sorry as I am. I shouldn't have. I know it, but I thought he loved me." Her voice broke. "And now he's probably off somewhere with his buddies talking up his conquest."

Knowing Duncan, that was a distinct possibility. "I'm sorry."

"Yeah, well, you were right, okay? And here you are with the perfect boyfriend—"

Ava squeezed Britt even tighter. "He's not."

"What do you mean?" Brittany pulled away and peered into Ava's eyes. "Mr. Amazing... isn't?"

"Here's something that might sound familiar. I haven't heard from Seth since Friday night. No calls, no texts, and he seems to have vanished."

"You have got to be kidding me."

"I wish," Ava whispered on a hiccup.

"But that's... crazy."

"I know."

"*You* didn't have sex, did you?"

"No." She sighed. "Just some amazing kisses that made me feel like the Fourth of July fireworks were exploding just for us. We danced in the park, Britt, to music only in our heads. I don't know what happened after that."

"Men are jerks and idiots."

Ava couldn't think of any evidence to dispute that hypothesis.

"Get out the ice cream. We'll drown it in cookies. Watch a chick flick."

Did she have to? She wanted to go in her room, shut the door, and cry her eyes out all by herself. She didn't want a pity party with Brittany.

But Britt pulled the meat cleaver out of the drawer and started smashing double chocolate cookies as though they were Duncan's fingers.

It wasn't all about Ava. Her cousin needed her. She put a hand out to stop the carnage. "I think that's enough crumbs for ice cream topping."

Britt angled her head, cleaver still in the air. "You might be right. But more would be better." She gave a couple of more whacks than handed the weapon to Ava. "Feels good. Want to give it a try?"

"No. Thanks, anyway. I'll get changed and then we can watch that movie. You pick the title."

In her room, Ava shimmied out of her narrow skirt and lacy top. Britt had the right idea. It might only be four in the afternoon, but it was time for sleepwear. They'd follow the ice cream with popcorn and movies until midnight.

And tomorrow morning, Ava would march down to the food forest and demand answers from Seth Donahue. He worked regular hours. He couldn't evade her there.

eth was a little ahead on the project, thanks to Ava's help, so Wade had no trouble letting him take a few days off. But now what? He couldn't keep three kids cooped up in the apartment for long... but how could he break this news to Ava? The way Bridgeview worked, if anyone saw them, she'd know within five minutes.

She'd be disappointed in him. Angry. She'd walk away.

She was going to, anyway. That a good girl like her had given a loser like him a second glance at all was, in itself, a miracle. He definitely wasn't worthy of her, no matter the delusions he'd been feeding himself.

Best to get it over with. Rip the comforting bandage off.

But he couldn't do it. Call him a coward, but something deep inside clung to the hope that she'd understand.

She wouldn't understand. Or, rather, she would. She'd see the evidence of his past they'd rarely spoken of. Beatrice and Peyton were one thing. They were in his life through no fault of his own. Leo was something else entirely.

Maybe Sadie was right, and Seth should go down to Pasco and see for himself how Eliza and John interacted with Beatrice and Peyton. He didn't want to invite the four of them to their house, though. He needed a bit of space to evaluate. He used to go camping with his buddies. Maybe he could borrow a bit of extra gear and get his motley family out of Spokane for a few days.

Peyton came out of the girls' bedroom rubbing sleep out of her eyes, her hair tousled, and dropped onto the wood floor beside Leo. She got three blocks stacked before Leo knocked them over, chortling with glee.

The sound shifted something inside of Seth.

"He's so cute." Peyton looked over at Seth. "I always wanted a baby brother."

"So you've said."

She stacked them again. Leo tumbled them again. Then she nestled beside Seth on the sofa. "Are we going to Violet's house today?"

"Not today. I'm taking a few days off work."

Peyton angled a look up at him. "How come?"

"I have some stuff to figure out. Having Leo come live with us changes things."

"Like now you don't want me and Beatrice anymore, because Leo is littler and cuter?"

Her words pierced his soul. He tugged her close. "That's definitely not what I'm thinking."

"Okay." She burrowed her face against his chest. "I miss Mommy and Daddy."

"I know, pumpkin. Me, too."

"But my mommy wasn't your mommy. Right?"

"That's true, but I had a mom, too, remember? She died

when I was a teenager. Then my dad married your mom and you two were born."

"Everybody's mom dies."

Seemed like it some days. Seth hadn't had time to mourn Diana. Not that he'd loved her as he should have, but her life and death had changed his trajectory. Her life would forever be tangled with his, and he needed time to process.

He messed up Peyton's hair, not that anyone would be able to tell. "Hey, do you like camping?"

"I don't know? What is it?"

"Let me see if I can make it happen. I need to make a few phone calls." Even with borrowing gear, this was a crazy idea, but now that it had come to mind, he had to try.

"I want breakfast." Peyton wiggled off the sofa.

"There's cereal."

Seth watched her trudge into the kitchen while Leo crawled after her. Seth did a mental sweep of anything on the floor the baby could reach. He pulled out his phone and gave Jared a call. Before long, he'd rounded up a second tent and a pair of sleeping bags with a promise to stop by for a longer visit with Jared and Billie sometime soon.

By the time Beatrice made an appearance, Seth had his plan in place.

⌒ ‧

HE'D BE at the food forest soon, wouldn't he?

Ava tried not to be too obvious with looking around as she picked the strawberries. They might not be the best choice in a permaculture bed because encroaching grass threatened to choke out the fragile runners.

She tucked the berries in the shade and went to work on the weeds. By the time she'd cleaned up one of the long rows it had become clear that Seth wasn't coming to work today.

Ava sat back on her heels as the niggling gave way to full-fledged worry. Maybe it wasn't all about her. Maybe something terrible had happened to him or one of the girls. She needed to get over herself and knock on his door. He'd have an explanation. He'd kiss her fears away.

Right?

Still, she stubbornly weeded for another half hour before she heard Olivia and Theodore outside next door. Their daddy would be at work — Wade was a biologist for Fish and Wildlife — but their mama would be home with the children. Since Seth worked for Wade, it stood to reason that Rebekah would know what was going on.

Ava dusted off her gloves before removing them and tucking them in the edge of her berry-picking basket. Then she wandered next door, pretending a casual ease she didn't feel in the slightest.

"Good morning, Ava! Wow, looks like the berries are doing well," Rebekah greeted her.

"They look great and taste the same. Would you like some of these?"

"Oh, no. You spent all that time picking. I'll get out there in a couple of days and get the next round, unless you have plans for them."

"Go for it." Ava had always loved the developing food forest, but it had lost its luster today with Seth absent. "Hey, I wondered if you knew where Seth was. Doesn't he usually work here on Mondays?"

Rebekah smirked but it faded away quickly, her eyes searching Ava's. "He called Wade yesterday and arranged to take a few days off. He's ahead on the project anyway, and he said something had come up."

Ava's mouth opened, but since her thoughts refused to line up into words, she closed it again.

"I take it he hasn't confided in you."

"No. He has not."

"I'm sorry you had to find out this way."

"But I don't know anything." Frustration spilled out of Ava. "What's so big he wouldn't tell me? We went out on Friday and everything was great."

What a dope she was. She saw everything through rose-colored glasses. Seth had a past? Well, it was history. He was redeemed now. Seth felt responsible for his two sisters and wanted to keep them permanently? Well, good for him stepping up to the plate for family. It might not be how Ava had planned her life, but she couldn't fault him for too much caring.

Or could she?

Because it was clear where she landed in his priority list. Below his sisters. Below his job. Below whatever random thing that had come up in his life this time.

Ava couldn't build a relationship based on landing in fourth or tenth or hundredth place. It felt like her heart was splitting in two, but she'd get over it. Get over him.

God had a Mr. Perfectly Right out there for her. She didn't need to settle for a guy who obviously wasn't ready to settle down and take a relationship seriously. Was a phone call too hard? How about a text? Or, you know, how about walking up a flight of stairs and knocking on her door?

Rebekah still stared at her with sympathy oozing from her gaze. "I'm sorry, Ava."

"Yeah. Me, too." Ava marched down the porch steps then turned back. "Why do guys need to be such jerks?"

"There's usually more than meets the eye."

Ava brushed the words aside. She knew that. Of course, she did. "They have the English language at their disposal, same as women."

Of course, Seth's car wasn't in the parking lot when she returned to Bridgeview Manor.

SETH DROVE into the campground beside Lake Wallula and soon secured a campsite. Leo had slept the entire two hours since they'd left Spokane.

Beatrice stood with her arms crossed and surveyed the campground. "I want to be by the lake."

"It's too dangerous with Leo," Seth reminded her.

"I liked it better without him around."

"Beatrice!" Peyton got right in her sister's face, saving Seth the bother. "That's not very nice. He's such a cute baby."

"*You're* a baby." Beatrice shoved at her sister.

Peyton burst into tears.

Seth set Leo's car seat on the ground with the baby still strapped in. He needed to get those tents up, and now. Not that anything would really contain Leo but four solid walls. What had Seth been thinking that he could manage three kids camping by a lake? Or anywhere? At any time?

He'd call Eliza in the morning, or maybe they'd just drop by and see what happened.

Somehow, he got through the day, ordering pizza delivery after a couple of hours of playing in the water with the three kids. Leo loved it and kept Seth busy scooping pebbles out of his mouth. Thankfully the tent he'd borrowed from Jared was big enough for Leo's pack-and-play as well as Seth's sleeping mat. He tucked the exhausted baby in bed at the regular time and silence reigned.

Then Seth pulled out graham crackers, chocolate, and marshmallows and taught the girls how to make s'mores. Even Beatrice seemed to be having a good time, despite herself.

"Time for bed, girls."

"The sun's still up," reasoned Beatrice.

"Not for long." Seth pointed toward the evening glow on the nearby river. "And we've got a busy day tomorrow."

Beatrice hiked her eyebrows, but he was saved from replying by Peyton's sleepy, "I like camping."

The next morning, he bundled up all three kids and took them to a pancake house for breakfast before looking up Eliza and John's address. He pulled up to the front of the house, turned off the ignition, and looked in the rearview mirror. "Do you know where we are?"

"Aunt Eliza's house!" chirruped Peyton from the middle seat.

Seth angled so he could see Beatrice, who stared out at the house. "Why are we here? Are you giving us away because you like Leo better?"

Guilt stabbed Seth's heart. "Nope. I know you two haven't seen them in a while, and I want to make sure you always know your mom's family. They're your family, too."

Beatrice looked him in the mirror, tears welling. "I promise to be good."

"I promise you're coming back to the campground with me. And back to Bridgeview tomorrow."

"Okay."

Seth unbuckled Leo while the girls waited on the sidewalk, and then they all walked toward the house. Together.

17

*D*o you have time to help me weed Nonna's garden?"

Ava's cousin Jasmine was on the phone. Jasmine, who had a business to run plus a toddler to chase. Why was she also enabling Nonna's garden, when it was obvious it was way too much work for the elderly woman to manage on her own?

But it wasn't like Ava had any better plans for the day. Not when Seth's car hadn't returned for two days. Yes, Ava had kept a close watch on the parking lot from her bedroom window.

"Sure. Why not?"

"Great! Meet you over there. Seems like ages since we've had a good visit. Wear sunscreen."

Yeah, yeah. Jasmine needed to mother someone else.

Ava waited twenty minutes to give Jasmine time to arrive before her, then walked the two blocks. Nonna sat in the covered patio area with little Lillian playing in a gated-off corner nearby.

"Hi, Nonna." Ava bent and air-kissed both her grand-mother's cheeks.

"Ava Elisabetta. You look well."

Nonna's eyesight must be failing. Ava had barely slept a wink in several nights now, and the mirror told her she looked anything but well. "So do you." She smiled at Nonna then scanned the backyard. "I'm here to help Jas."

"Over here!" her cousin called. "I need a hand staking up these tomato plants."

Ava pulled on her gardening gloves and wended her way between the rows of raised beds. "Just tell me what to do."

"That's my specialty." Jasmine gave her a grin. "How's the job search going?"

"Southside Elementary called yesterday to say they'd hired a third-grade teacher with musical training, and they're going to run their program in-house."

"Oh, no."

Ava glanced toward the patio where Nonna was making googly-eyes at her great-granddaughter. "I've been thinking about applying to a ritzy girls' school back east. There is one in New York offering a position I'd match."

"No way."

"Yes way. What's there for me here in Spokane? No one wants me."

Jasmine straightened and met Ava's gaze. "Your family is here. We all want you."

"That doesn't pay the bills." It wasn't super fulfilling, either.

"No, I guess not, but everything will fall into place soon. You'll see."

"I've been teaching three years and still can't find full-time work."

"Have you thought about going for a regular position instead?"

Ava sighed. "Yes, I've thought about it, but music is in my blood. I don't know how to excise it."

"I did a job I didn't love for a few years before going for my dream."

Jasmine had had her own massage therapy clinic but hated being locked up in a building. Now she operated Bridgeview Backyards with Ava's brother, Peter, and a handful of student helpers. They gardened in over a dozen nearby yards and sold the produce through subscriptions.

"I know, Jas. I just thought I had a realistic dream. Turns out I didn't. And I know it hasn't been easy for you and Peter, either. At least not when you guys had to buy Basil out."

"And run the business with one less lead hand. Yes, it's been difficult at times. Hopefully my big brother has learned a thing or two since his jail time."

Ava recalled Basil's sardonic company at Alex and Marley's wedding. She doubted Basil had learned a thing.

"He's doing well at the Fireweed in Seattle. Shift manager. I keep hoping he'll come home. Back to Bridgeview, back to Jesus, and back to working with Peter and me."

"That would be great." Ava didn't want to talk about Basil.

"But enough about my brother." Jasmine glanced toward the back of the house and lowered her voice. "I hear you went on a hot date with Seth Donahue. Then why are you talking about leaving Spokane?"

Maybe Ava didn't want to talk about Seth, either. "Because he ghosted me."

"You're kidding." Jasmine searched her face. "Okay, you're not. What happened?"

"Amazing date on Friday. Now it's Tuesday and I haven't seen him. I don't think anyone has." He'd said Dan Ranta was watching the girls that night. Maybe Dan or Dixie would know what was up, but Ava hated asking. She hated looking and sounding pathetic. The person she should be hearing from was Seth himself.

"That's terrible."

"Tell me. I have rotten taste in guys. I think I'll give up dating until I'm thirty."

"You'd think that was ancient or something."

Ava shrugged and reached for another tomato stake. "I just need a break. I obviously can't trust myself."

"I'm sorry you're hurting, cuz."

"How did you forgive Nathan?"

"Well, it was clear he'd turned over a new leaf. That he was truly sorry for the way he'd treated me in college and the way he'd lived in California after he left here. But mostly because God forgave him and challenged me to do the same. To stop pretending Nathan had hurt me more than he'd hurt God."

That sounded so mature. Ava didn't have that in her. Not today. Besides, she and Seth didn't have a whole history together like Jasmine and Nathan had from high school and college. They'd only met a month ago. Only gone on one date.

How could the man who'd cradled her close and danced with her in the butterfly garden and showered her with kisses turn around and ghost her the very next day? It just didn't add up.

Ava doubted there was anything Seth could say now to restore her trust in him.

"BEATRICE! PEYTON!" Eliza erupted from the brick house and flew toward them, embracing one girl then the other. Beatrice hung back, while Peyton clung to her aunt's neck. "Hi, Seth. To what do I owe the honor of this visit?"

"You're their aunt," he said simply. "Just because their mom died doesn't mean you shouldn't ever see them again."

"And who's this little guy?" She chucked Leo under the chin.

"My son."

Eliza angled her head and examined the baby and then Seth. "What a surprise."

Wasn't that an understatement? "Yes. Do you have a few minutes?"

"Um, sure. Come on in. I'll put on a coffee. John's at the office, and I have almost an hour before I need to be in a meeting myself."

Seth glanced at Beatrice and caught the relief on her face. The girls followed their aunt, and he brought up the rear. The house was large. Immaculate. So unlike his apartment. Seth felt a vice tighten around his heart. *Please, God, show me what's best for the girls. Truly best.*

Eliza led them into an expansive white and granite kitchen. "Would you girls like to play a video game?"

"Sure!" Peyton rocked on her heels.

"I'll set you up here in the family room while I talk to your brother."

There was something off about Eliza. She wasn't

meeting anyone's gaze for more than a second or two. This house might be big enough to take in two little girls, but would they be allowed to play and make it messy? Maybe Eliza knew a way to keep things picked up with mind control or something. Maybe she'd teach Seth the trick.

She turned on the coffee pot then settled across from Seth at the bar-height table. "Did your attorney mention hearing from me?"

Ice formed in Seth's belly. "When was this?"

"Just this morning."

He hadn't checked his email before driving into the city. "Why don't you tell me what you told her?"

Eliza glanced toward the girls and twisted her hands together. "John filed for divorce on Friday. He's involved with a young, pretty thing from the office."

"Oh, no. I'm so sorry." Seemed like no one could keep a relationship together these days.

"Since Lori died..." Eliza dabbed at her eyes with a tissue. "My heart hasn't been into things here, I guess. I felt so sure I should take care of the girls, but with John it was always something we'd discuss tomorrow or next week. Or we'd see how it went. Now I know why he refused to make a decision."

"That... explains a lot." Seth's mind reeled with the implications.

"I know. I'm so sorry. I just don't know what to do. John wants to list the house this week. I don't want to buy him out and stay living here with all the memories. I don't know what I'll do. I guess I'm in no position to be taking on Lori's daughters."

"Her death... and my dad's... such a big shock to us all."

"How are the girls doing, really? They look well. You

must be taking good care of them."

"It hasn't been easy, especially in the past few days since I found out I had a son whose mother passed away. Peyton says all moms just die. I hope I can set her mind at ease on that one before she's an adult, or she'll never want to have kids of her own."

Eliza sniffled then reached for a tissue. "I don't know how you do it."

"Look after three kids? It's not easy. I don't have a degree or even a permanent job."

"I wish I could help."

"You've got plenty on your plate, too, by the sounds of it. We'll manage. We live in a great neighborhood where people pitch in and help each other. The girls are making friends." It sounded so much better than reality felt. "There's a solid community church and school, too." A church he'd planned to dig his roots into. But was that wise with Leo? Everything had changed.

He had to set Ava aside along with all the dreams and hopes she'd stirred in him. Disappointment pooled deep, alerting him to the awareness he'd really hoped Eliza would prove to be absolutely perfect to take over the girls, and he could relinquish them to her without a single worry. That was not the case.

A glance into the other room showed the game paused and the girls whispering with their heads together.

"That sounds perfect. I envy you that kind of place. John and I have lived here for eighteen years, and I barely know any of my neighbors. I guess it doesn't matter anymore since I'm moving out."

Beautiful surroundings didn't make a marriage. Good to know. "What are you going to do?"

"I don't know." She wrung her hands together. "I need a fresh start away from Pasco. Away from John and *her*."

"You're a teacher, right? Why not move to Spokane? There must be job openings there." Too late he remembered that Ava didn't have a permanent gig, but then she was looking for something very specific. "Then you could see the girls more."

Her face brightened. "I hadn't thought of that as an option. I've just been wallowing in this whole thing with John. To be honest, I didn't think you'd want me anywhere near them."

"It doesn't have to be all or nothing. Maybe not for either of us."

She looked at him with wide eyes. "What, exactly, are you proposing?"

What? No. He shook his head vehemently. "I'm not proposing anything between you and me." The woman was at least ten years his senior, and he barely knew her.

"Oh. I thought you meant... never mind. My mind's such a mess these days. But living nearby, sharing some of the care of my nieces... that would give me something to look forward to when all the dust clears here. I'd never thought of moving to a different school system, but it can't hurt to have a look and see if there are any openings that fit my experience."

On his lap, Leo stiffened and began grunting. Great timing. "Any place I can take this kid to change his diaper?"

"Sure. There's a powder room just through the family room."

Seth tucked the baby under his arm football-style and strode between the girls and the television they weren't watching. "Good game?"

Beatrice wrinkled her nose. "Leo stinks."

"Thanks for letting me know." Seth winked at her.

"It's a hard game," Peyton whispered with a glance toward her aunt.

"We were trying to listen to you talk," Beatrice added.

"Still worried about me leaving you here?"

She nodded, looking down and twisting the hem of her top.

"Don't be. You're coming with me. We're stuck with each other until you're a grownup."

"Really?" Peyton bounced toward him but stopped and waved her hand in front of her nose.

"Really. I'm going to change this kid. You two go talk to your aunt for a few minutes, then we'll head back to the campground."

"I'm hungry," Peyton informed him. "Can we stop for a burger?"

Why not? It was only money. If he needed to dig into the funds from the sale of their parents' house to raise his sisters with, so be it. They had to survive meanwhile.

He came back into the kitchen a few minutes later to see the girls flanking their aunt and looking at something on her phone. "What's up?"

"Aunt Eliza wants to go for lunch with us," Beatrice announced. "There's a fancy burger place, she says. Can we go there?"

Seth looked at Eliza. "Uh..."

"My treat. I'll just call and postpone my appointment to later. Not a biggie."

"If you're sure."

"Absolutely. I don't want to miss a minute of this time with my nieces."

18

*H*er phone chimed with an incoming text minutes before dance class began on Thursday afternoon. Seth? After five and a half days of radio silence? No way was she opening that right now and losing all the focus she needed for teaching. She'd rather pitch her phone across the room.

He was probably pulling his sisters out of class. That would be the message. Then she'd be back to her earlier plans for fourteen kids, not sixteen. It was irritating. Annoying. Aggravating... but she'd get over it. She'd get over *him*. In five years, maybe. Not this week. Not when he'd ditched her without a word.

Kids were already starting to arrive. Sebastian Ferguson. Tieri Amato. Violet Sheridan. Sabrina and Manny Ramirez. Beatrice and Peyton...

What were they doing here? Maybe she should have read Seth's text after all.

Ava was an adult. Whatever had happened had nothing to do with these two girls. She could smile and treat them like two of the group, like every other week. The smile might even be easy — she still had sixteen dancers.

Peyton darted over and gave her a swift hug around the middle. "I missed you!"

Where was the appropriate response? Ava patted the girl's back and called the class to order. At the edge of the group, Beatrice pulled Peyton aside and gave her a fierce talking-to. Both girls glanced at Ava then focused back on each other. Peyton's shoulders slumped, and tears filled her eyes.

Ava simply could not go there. "Let's start with our stretches." Good thing there were still two months before the performance, since she doubted she could teach them anything new today. Not as distracted as she was.

An hour later, she couldn't have told anyone what they'd done in class, but the time had passed, and the kids dashed out to their waiting rides. Would Seth be coming inside? He usually did, but his half-sisters left the studio with their friends.

Ava let out a long breath. She needed to pull together long enough to tidy the space and lock up behind herself. She'd open that text in the privacy of her apartment. Brittany would still be at work for another hour, which gave Ava enough time to cry *and* make dinner.

Seth's car wasn't in the church parking lot, not that she expected it to be, twenty minutes after class let out.

She walked home, avoiding checking for his car on the other side of Bridgeview Manor. Up three flights of stairs, right past his apartment door to her own. She poured a glass of iced tea then sat down in her favorite chair, scrunching her eyes shut.

Lord, why am I so terrified to read this? I know it's a Dear

John letter, or Dear Jane or whatever it's called when the guy ditches the girl. I've known it was over for days now, but I still don't want to read the stark truth. He was so amazing, Lord.

Except for all the ways he didn't measure up. His less than exemplary past. His lack of a job or even a direction. His custody of his two half-sisters.

No, it was probably a good thing he was calling it off now. She should never have gotten involved in the first place. She'd known from the get-go that he wasn't Mr. Perfectly Right, but she'd played with fire anyway. Not to the degree Brittany had — Ava took a few seconds to pray that her cousin wasn't pregnant — but she'd still allowed herself to fall for Mr. Completely Wrong.

So, she'd get over him and someday — *please, God* — she'd meet the right guy, and he'd be so totally worth waiting for.

Okay. She could open the text now.

Sorry for disappearing on you.

Uh huh. Nice start, buddy.

Something rather major came up, and I wound up having to go out of town for a few days. I'd like a chance to explain.

Like there was anything at all he could say to clear this up. What, he'd been in an accident, bonked his head, and gotten amnesia? Sure, she'd fall for that. Not.

Ava chewed on her lip for a moment before tapping a reply. *No need to explain. Don't worry about it.* She thought a bit longer before finishing her text. *It was fun, but we're not really on the same page, so let's forget Friday ever happened.*

She hit *send* before she could second-guess herself then slammed her phone onto the sofa and stacked all three throw cushions on top of it. First, she'd eat a dozen cookies, then she'd make a gourmet dinner for Brittany and herself. Meanwhile, she'd crank some music so she wouldn't even hear if her phone received a text. It would also cover the random sounds of the crying baby that had returned after a few days of quiet.

Ignorance was bliss. Or something like that.

⌒‿⌒

SETH JIGGLED LEO, but the kid would not stop howling. The baby refused food, wore a dry diaper, and had too short a nap. Beatrice walked through the living room with both hands over her ears, glowering at the pair of them. Even Peyton seemed to have forgotten that Leo was cute.

He wasn't cute.

Not right now.

His phone dinged, and he surged toward it, startling Leo into a louder wail.

Ava.

His breathing stuttered. It had been totally chicken of him to text fifteen minutes before her class. He'd known it, but did it anyway. And he'd made his sisters promise not to mention Leo or their trip to Pasco to anyone, even Ms. Ava.

He read the text three times, feeling the sting of her rejection deeper each time. She didn't even know what had happened, but she'd decided they were all wrong for each other?

Seth knew they were. He'd been going to explain and let her down as gently as he could. The whole it's-not-you-it's-me thing was so totally true it was nearly laughable. How had he let his own desires get ahead of wisdom?

Yes, old things had passed away, and all things had become new. Except for the things that hadn't, like his son.

Seth was never going to be free of his past, no matter what the Bible said. Even guys like Abraham and Moses and David faced the consequences of their sins for the rest of their lives. Seth wasn't getting off scot free, either.

But he hadn't expected Ava to take the initiative to dump him before he'd even proved to her what a mess he was. Just a few days of silence — okay, he shouldn't have blocked her out, maybe, but what else could he have done? Phoned her and said, 'oh, by the way, I have a child? Just found out. No biggie, right?'

It didn't matter how they'd reached this place of breaking up. It was for the best. He'd get over her, as she was obviously already over him. Maybe she went around dancing in the park and kissing guys all the time. Maybe it truly had meant nothing to her.

No. She'd been all in.

But it still didn't matter. Leo was a bucket of ice water dumped over Seth's head, a reminder he could not out-run his past.

He texted back. *Thanks for understanding.*

She hadn't understood, but it seemed the right thing to say.

Meanwhile, Seth needed to figure out his life. He needed a sitter by Monday who could take all three kids. He just had a few more weeks of working for Wade. He'd get through those somehow, even if he spent almost every penny of his earnings on childcare.

Right now, all his hopes were pinned on Eliza coming through for him. If she moved to Spokane and helped pick up the slack with the girls, he might stand a chance of surviving the next few years.

It seemed God had deserted him. Ava certainly had. But maybe Eliza wouldn't.

⁓

AVA PUSHED her grocery cart through Main Market Co-op. After Brittany's baking jag last weekend, they were low on flour, sugar, and everything else. Worst of all, they'd consumed all the chocolate chips. Ava squatted to pick up a large bag of flour from the bottom shelf then heard a baby chortle nearby. Peyton's voice giggled.

Peyton?

Ava stilled, craning to hear. A second later Peyton bounded around the end of the aisle and stopped dead when she saw Ava. Then her face brightened, and she dashed toward her.

Somehow Ava got the flour in the cart before the child slammed into her. "Hi, Ms. Ava!"

"Hey, Peyton." But her gaze was fixed on the grocery cart turning down the end of the aisle. Pushed by Seth. With a baby facing him in the cart's child seat.

Seth.

A baby.

He jerked to a stop, his eyes widening. He looked from her to the babbling baby and back to Ava.

Well. That explained a lot. Except it didn't. Did everyone in Bridgeview know besides her? How could he... what on earth...

Ava grabbed her cart handle and shoved forward, away from him. She was close to the end of the aisle. She'd just—

"Ava, wait!"

Not a chance. She didn't even need these groceries that badly. She left the cart in the next aisle and dashed toward the doors. She'd come back later. Or go to a different store. Or send Brittany. It didn't matter. There was no stinking way she was staying in the co-op and smiling and nodding at Seth.

Seth had a baby.

That's who she'd been hearing at times in the building. Had to be.

He had a *baby*.

When was he going to tell her? Yesterday when he texted? She hadn't blocked his number. He could have sent another text. *Oh, by the way, I have a baby*.

She'd been hearing the evidence on and off since their date. Had he hired a sitter that evening and not bothered to tell her? Just kissed her like she was the most amazing woman he'd ever met while conveniently neglecting to tell her. *He. Had. A. Baby?*

Ava jumped in her car, not bothering to look back toward the doors. Likely he wasn't there, anyway, trying to stop her. She drove straight to her parents' house and slammed on the brakes. In seconds, she was inside her mother's kitchen, bawling her eyes out.

Like a baby.

But she deserved to cry. He'd humiliated her. Hurt her. Led her on. This was not okay. No one else might understand, but her mama would.

"Oh, honey." Mom's hands stroked Ava's back. "What is it? Tell me."

And everything tumbled out. How she and Seth had met. How they'd worked together at the food forest. How he'd stepped up to care for his half-sisters after their parents' deaths. How she'd fallen for him even though she'd known better. After all, he had nothing to offer her.

How he'd ghosted her.

And then they'd parted ways.

And then the baby.

Ava still couldn't believe her own memory, but she couldn't unsee that chortling baby, kicking his chubby little legs in the grocery cart.

"Mom, I don't know what to do!"

"It sounds like it has all been done already."

"I know, but..." Ava hiccupped.

"You love him?"

"I thought so, but I didn't really know him." Clearly.

Mom tilted Ava away enough to look into her eyes. "My precious child, have you asked God for wisdom?"

"Sort of?" Or maybe she'd just told Him what she felt like and what she was going to next.

"Then let us pray now." Mom held her tight and laid it all out before God. She asked for wisdom. She asked for guidance and blessing and a job for Seth. For peace and strength for Ava. She prayed comfort for Beatrice and Peyton. She prayed for the baby. She prayed through all of Ava's sniffles until the bitterness began to subside and something like peace began to settle. And then she said, "Amen."

"Amen."

Ava jumped at her dad's deep voice. How had he snuck in without her hearing him? And what had he overheard? Hopefully enough she didn't need to tell her sordid tale again.

"I love you, princess." Dad gave her a side-hug. "If your

mother hadn't already asked God to handle everything, I'd promise to kick the young man's knees in."

Ava managed a smile at her sweet daddy's show of support. "That means a lot, Papa, but no."

"You know, when I went courting your mother, I didn't have a career, either. Raimondo was eager to become a pilot, but I had no such ambitions. Going to college wasn't expected of us boys, and I have no idea what career I would have chosen if I'd gone. A contractor friend of my papa's hired me to help paint some houses with him that summer, and I liked it well enough I stayed on. Eventually I took over that part of his business."

Ava'd heard this story, but today it sounded a little different. "You didn't always want to be a painter?"

He scoffed. "How could that be anyone's life dream?" His blue eyes warmed as he looked at his wife. "This woman, your mama, she was my dream. I am only thankful I could earn a living enough to care for my Betta. To provide a home and food for our three children. God has blessed me, Ava Elizabeth. Make no mistake. There is no greater honor than to care for one's family. A man — or a woman — need not have a degree to experience that blessing."

What was he saying? Ava opened her mouth to ask, but Dad held up his hand.

"I am thankful we could provide a college education for Peter, for you, and now for Dafne, but only because you wished for it. You had that dream to be a teacher. But if you had desired to become a mechanic — or a house painter like your papa — that would have been fine, too. Do not look down upon a man who works with his hands to take care of his family. It is an honor. Always an honor."

"Yes, Daddy." Was she guilty of looking down on Seth because he hadn't finished college? Or was she only sad on his behalf because he'd accomplished three years and only needed one more to graduate?

Because her father was right. It took many different jobs to keep an economy running. Seth didn't need college. He needed a job... but she didn't have one to offer him.

*S*eth couldn't get away from Ava's relatives in this neighborhood. Rebekah had suggested Fran Amato as someone who operated a daycare from home, believing there were vacant spots since Rebekah was home for the summer with Olivia and Theodore.

And Fran turned out to be one of Ava's cousins. There must be dozens of them. All the more reason to move out of Bridgeview as soon as he could, but that wouldn't be this week.

The three kids were ensconced at Fran's daycare. Her daughter, Tieri, was between his sisters in age, while her son, Luca, was a little younger. Beatrice and Violet hadn't been getting along well, anyway, so hopefully this would work until Seth's temp job ended and school started again

Ava hadn't come down to the food forest while he worked. He hadn't seen her for ten days now, not since that afternoon at Main Market Co-op when she'd dashed out, leaving a fully loaded grocery cart in the middle of the aisle.

And he hadn't contacted her. What was the point?

Explanations would only take him so far, but not far enough. She was better off without him. Not only did he firmly believe that himself, she obviously did, too.

Seth shook off the thoughts and glanced up at the approach of a man who looked to be a bit older than him. The guy stuck out his hand. "Seth Donahue? I'm Jacob Riehl. Wade asked me to stop by and introduce you to that solar-powered pump."

"Yes, that's me." Seth shook his hand. "Nice to meet you. I didn't think there was that much to installing the pump, but Wade wanted to be sure, I guess." He'd examined the schematic. It was mostly plug-and-play. It kind of bugged him that Wade didn't think he was capable of installing it on his own. Just because he didn't have a diploma to prove he could read.

"There isn't." Jacob grinned. "But something Wade is known for around here is making sure people get to know their neighbors. And since I'm an architectural engineer with a specialty in solar design, I guess I'm the resident expert."

That was a thing? "I see."

"My wife and I and our girls live next door to Dan and Dixie. I think I've seen you over there a time or two?"

"Could be. I've known them a while." Might as well dump everything out. It wasn't like everybody didn't already know. "I have custody of my two half-sisters, who are ten and eight. And my son will be a year old in September."

"You're lucky there's just one of him. Our twins are about the same age as your little guy. Oh, my goodness. We had no idea what to expect, but trouble's name is Indigo and Anya."

No question of where his baby's mother was? That was a

relief. An easy enough question to answer, in a way. *His mother died.* But it opened the door to more questions, and Seth had a pump to install. That was what he was getting paid for here, not yakking or therapy.

Seth scuffed a boot toward the trench he'd hand-dug. "I've laid the water line in the bottom of that. And over here is the pond. I got the liner in place yesterday." Now that would have been easier with a second set of hands, but he missed Ava's company far more than her assistance. She'd simply brightened his days just with her presence.

He missed her like crazy.

Jacob circled the pond, eyeing the nearby trees, then pointed out the spot where the pump should be installed. Exactly where Seth had figured. But when Jacob began to explain how the solar parts worked, Seth peppered him with questions. Then, while the pond filled, Seth moved on to questions about advancing to architectural engineering — and especially solar — not that he had any designs to go to school for several more years. If he'd once had dreams, they'd been crushed and kicked to the curb.

"You should look into electrical work," Jacob said. "You've got a good understanding of circuitry."

"I don't know anyone hiring, especially newbies." Hadn't Wade made a suggestion about an electrician? Oh, yeah. A man who was related to Ava. Everyone around here was. "I'm honestly not sure what my long-term plans are. We might be moving."

"Moving a lot is hard on kids. Not that I know from experience."

Hard to disagree with, but it also didn't change the facts.

Jacob snapped his fingers. "Franco Santoro is a licensed

electrician with his own business. I should hook you up with him and see if he's got an opening."

Santoro. "No, thank you."

"Why not, man? He's a good Christian man and pays decently. Related to half the people around here. His daughter, Fran, even runs a neighborhood daycare."

"She's watching the kids right now." He eyed Jacob. "Are you related to them, too?"

"The Santoros?" Jacob grinned. "Not me. Not my wife, either. But they're good friends of ours. Let me call Franco. Give yourself a chance."

Seth shook his head. "It really wouldn't work out." If Jacob didn't know why, he might be the only person in the community. "I'm not sure I'm cut out to be an electrician. I've got one more year to become an engineer, and I have no idea when I could make that happen."

"You sure? I'm happy to make the introductions. You know what they say, right? It's not *what* you know, it's *who* you know."

Seth forced a grin. "I thought that was just in small towns."

Jacob chuckled. "Bridgeview has the same feel, trust me." He leaned over to look into the pond. "Looks like the pump is working well enough, and the float is in place to keep it from overflowing. Any other questions?"

He hadn't had any to start with. "No, thanks. I'll get the perimeter planting in over the rest of this week, then I think Wade has a few more odd tasks for me to do around here."

"And then you'll need a more permanent job."

Seth nodded, not meeting Jacob's gaze.

"Then let me spread the word."

The guy was persistent, but nothing good could come from staying in the neighborhood.

܀

"YOU GOING TO THE FIREWORKS DOWNTOWN?"

Ava eyed her sister. "No." Half the sparks flying around Riverside Park would be from starry-eyed couples sneaking kisses. Wasn't it just last year the fireworks had set something off between Alex and Marley? And here they were, happily married.

Maybe she should go. She might meet someone.

That was laughable.

"Would you like to hang out with Gavin so I could go?"

"Hot date?" Ava eyed her younger sister.

"Not a chance." Dafne laughed. "I'd like to go with some friends from college. *Girl*friends."

"Sure. Why not? Do you think he'd like to spend the night here with Britt and me?"

Dafne frowned. "Isn't she going? I thought she was dating what's-his-name."

"Duncan. And no, they broke up a couple of weeks ago." If it could be called breaking up when the guy had just never bothered to show his face again.

"Good. He's a total jerk."

"Yup."

Dafne sighed. "I bet Gavin would be thrilled to stay over. Peter has a blow-up mattress and sleeping bag I can probably borrow. Just don't let him stay up too late."

"Who, Peter?"

"Silly." Grinning, Daf smacked Ava's arm. "I owe you big time."

"I thought we'd decided not to keep score over Gav. He's my nephew. I love him."

"Thanks. I don't know what I'd do without you. Without Mom and Dad's support. I messed up so badly."

Ava pulled her sister into a hug. "You're forgiven. You know that, right? By God. By your family. By anyone who matters."

"Consequences remain. Not that I don't love my son. I do. Totally. It's such a weird place to be, but sometimes I can't help wishing I could be an average college student with her whole life in front of her."

"You do have that."

"I know. But it's not the same."

Ava searched Dafne's expression. "Granted. It doesn't usually get you down."

"There are days. I ran into Connor a few days ago. Free-as-a-bird Connor. He looked at Gavin for a few seconds before saying hi, then just walked away. It's not fair that I have all the responsibility, and he has none."

Connor Hamelin, Gavin's father, was the younger half-brother of Jasmine's husband, Nathan. He and Dafne had been teens when their son had been conceived, and he'd pushed hard for an abortion. Daf had run away from home in the dead of winter to evade him back then.

"Aw, sis. I'm sorry." Ava gave Dafne a hug. "If you and your friends want to go out for dinner, bring Gavin by in the late afternoon. Britt and I will have fun spoiling him."

"Thanks. You're the best." Dafne squished her back so tightly Ava couldn't breathe. "What's going on with Seth? Did you ever find out why he has a baby?"

"Sorry, sis, but I think we both know how babies happen."

"That's not what I meant." Daf rolled her eyes.

"I know. I... didn't ask him. I don't want to know. Besides, I think he moved out last weekend. His contract with Wade should be finished at the end of July, too."

Dafne's eyebrows rose as she searched Ava's face. "You should talk to him while you know where to find him. Get some closure."

"Believe me, I have all of that I can handle."

"I don't think it's called closure in that case."

"Yeah, well. It doesn't matter. I'm fine. Really."

"Got one question for you, and then I'll leave it."

Ava met her sister's gaze. "Yeah?"

"You keep telling me you love me. That you understand how life-altering mistakes happen. That you've forgiven me and support me."

Where was this going? Ava nodded cautiously.

"Seth has a story, too. I don't know what it is, but I know you're capable of getting past it. God's forgiveness is real. I know that better than many people do, but the forgiveness and support of those around us makes a huge difference in day-to-day life. Give it a try?"

The apartment door swung open, and Brittany came in, gaze wobbling between them. "Am I interrupting something?"

"Not at all," Ava said quickly.

Dafne turned to their cousin. "Do you believe in forgiveness?"

"In theory, yes. But sometimes it is hard to do. It's also harder to forgive yourself than other people. What's the context?"

Ava tried not to stare at Brittany. Was she getting over the fiasco with Duncan?

"The context is Ava forgiving Seth."

Brittany crossed her arms and raised her eyebrows. "But not getting back together."

Dafne shrugged. "Two separate topics. The forgiveness needs to happen regardless."

"Well, maybe. Someone wise once said that holding onto bitterness is like drinking poison and hoping the other person dies."

"I don't hope anyone dies," muttered Ava. A swift kick below the belt wouldn't go amiss, though.

Her phone rang. Whew, nice escape from this pointed conversation. She turned away and glanced at the screen, and her breath fled. Bridgeview Elementary. Had she gotten the fifth-grade teaching position?

"Hello, this is Ava Santoro speaking."

"Randi Nordstrom here. I'm sorry to be the one to tell you, but we had a last-minute application from someone moving to Spokane who has taught fifth grade for fourteen years. She has every credential we were looking for, and we've decided to hire her."

"Oh." All the breath whooshed out of Ava. "I see."

"Honestly, Ava, I understand why you applied, but you'd be wasted in a regular classroom. We would hate to lose you as our music and dance teacher."

"Thank you. But I need more hours."

"I know. I've put out the word, but I can't influence the choices other principals in the area make."

"I appreciate the thought. Thanks for letting me know." Ava tapped to end the call then turned slowly to face her sister and cousin. "I didn't get the full-time position."

Dafne frowned. "I didn't think you really wanted it."

"I didn't... but I do. I can't exist on point-six income forever."

"Isn't it handy I've got a good job?" Brittany smirked.

"I hate taking advantage of you."

Brittany hugged her. "Don't. Grace goes in all directions."

Well, hadn't her cousin had a breakthrough? Too bad the same thing was elusive for Ava. Maybe Seth had not only moved out of the building but outside of the school catchment area. Maybe Beatrice and Peyton wouldn't be in any of the schools she taught in come August. But they were still in Thursday's dance class, so that hope might be unfounded.

Is that what Ava really wished for? No. All she wanted was Seth, unencumbered by three kids. Especially a baby that actually belonged to him.

20

I love it!" yelled Peyton, leaning over the railing. "Can me and Bea have this amazing loft please-please-please?"

"Beatrice and I," corrected Eliza, but she was smiling as she turned to Seth. "That would leave the two bedrooms on the main floor for you and Leo. What do you think?"

Seth looked around, shaking his head in wonder. Just like that, Eliza had snapped up both sides of a duplex a few blocks up the hill from Bridgeview Elementary. She'd live in one half, and he and the kids would live in the other. The girls could freely move between the two units and enjoy the shared backyard.

"I don't know what to say."

"You're doing me a favor, too."

He guffawed as he set Leo on the floor. "How do you figure that?"

"I was at loose ends in Pasco, but it never occurred to me to pack up and move away from John. Then you put a bug in my ear to consider coming here, and everything fell into place in under a week. John decided to buy me out on the house, and I landed a teaching job."

She gave a little twirl that reminded Seth of Peyton. It was good for the girls to be near their mom's sister.

"And now I can help out with my nieces. Everything is just perfect."

Except for John, but Seth wasn't going to bring up her ex. If Eliza could move on, he wouldn't stand in her way. "I called my attorney and told her we'd worked everything out between us."

"I'm sorry you felt you needed to hire one."

Seth shrugged. "She helped me out pro bono, which was a huge relief. She and her husband have become friends." If he could remain friends with Ava's brother.

His gaze landed on Leo, and he lurched forward to pluck the baby off the third step to the loft.

Leo arched his back and screamed at being denied his freedom.

"My first purchase will be a baby gate. But at least he won't disturb the other residents of the apartment building anymore. Babies don't do well with neighbors on all sides."

Eliza chuckled and held out her hands for Leo, who went to her willingly. "He's such a sweetheart. And I'm a sound sleeper, so don't worry about me on the other side. We'll be fine."

"Seth!" yelled Peyton. "I think that tree is big enough to climb!"

He followed Eliza and Leo up to the loft. The space would be good for the girls, though they'd need drapes or a screen or something to block their view of the street beyond the two-story living room. There was even a full bath up there. He'd be okay with all their girlie paraphernalia corralled into their own space.

Now he crossed to the large window overlooking the backyard. "That is a great tree," he agreed. "You can give it a try if you like."

"Maybe we could have a treehouse like Violet?" Peyton turned her puppy-dog eyes on him.

"That will be up to your aunt."

"*Please*, Auntie Eliza!"

"We'll definitely consider it." She smiled at Peyton.

Seth slipped his arm around Beatrice's shoulders. "What do you think?"

"It's better than that stupid apartment."

He couldn't argue. "That's all I could find six weeks ago." Also all he could afford. He still wasn't sure how he could pay his rent to Eliza, but she kept insisting things would work out.

Beatrice nodded and turned into his chest. "I miss my mom."

"I know, sweetie." Seth rubbed her back. "I get it."

"I think it's funny that your house is just like ours, but backward!" Peyton said to Eliza. "What will you do with your loft?"

"I'm not sure. Maybe an art studio."

The little girl's eyes grew wide. "You're an artist *and* a teacher?"

"I wouldn't call myself an artist, but I like to play with paint."

"Me, too," Peyton breathed in awe.

Yes, creating a team with Eliza would be a vast improvement over raising these girls by himself. They'd talked in depth about who would be the primary caregiver and, because the girls never voiced desire for change, they'd decided to leave the arrangement.

If only finding common ground with Ava would be half as simple. Had she excised him from her mind, or did she have second thoughts? Should he try one more time?

Having a better place to live and Eliza's help with the girls made him feel like he had a better foundation. He still needed a decent job, though.

But there was a very real chance Ava wouldn't give him another chance. The look of disbelief — horror, even — on her face that day in Main Market Co-op was etched in his memory.

There'd be no forgiveness.

It could take years for the ache in his heart to fade.

⚬⚬⚬

"WE HAVE A BIG HOUSE!" exclaimed Peyton. "And we have a climbing tree, and my auntie lives next door! She got 'vorced and moved here."

Ava smiled at the little girl. It wasn't the child's fault her brother was a jerk. "I'm happy everything worked out for you, and I'm glad you're still in dance class."

"It's so much fun. My auntie says she'll bring Bea and me to church, too."

"Beatrice and I," corrected Ava. And did that mean Seth wouldn't be returning to Bridgeview Bible? Sounded like it. Guilt stabbed her heart. Was it her fault? Was she hindering his spiritual growth by not talking to him, not forgiving him?

It didn't mean they needed to get back together. It just

meant they could both move on, right? But it seemed he already had.

Ava's gaze hung up on the woman beside Beatrice at the door to the studio. Somehow she'd expected the girls' aunt to be old. Or at least older than she appeared.

Probably Seth would fall in love with her. Wouldn't that be just perfect for him? Two people who loved Beatrice and Peyton creating a united home. Yes, she was probably older than Seth, but not insurmountably so. She was pretty with her curly reddish hair, and Beatrice smiled up at her as they approached.

Yup. Perfect. *Put your game face on, Ava.*

"Hi. I'm Eliza Nelson, the girls' aunt. You must be Ava. I've heard so much about you."

"All good, I hope." Ava held out her hand. No way was she giving this woman any ammunition. "It's been a delight having the girls in class, so I'm glad to hear they'll be continuing on, though I hear they've moved."

Eliza smiled. "Not far, just up the hill a little. It's a great spot, since it's close enough to walk to Bridgeview Elementary. I'll be teaching there."

Ava's smile froze. "Fifth grade?"

"Why, yes! You're familiar with the school? Do you have a child there?"

"I'm a teacher, too. I rotate through several area elementary schools teaching music and dance. Including Bridgeview."

"Oh, how lovely."

Sure, lovely for Eliza Nelson, who'd stolen Ava's job *and* her boyfriend. Ava held her smile, though it might look more like a grimace by now. "All right, children. Find your spots. It's time for our warmup." She glanced back at Eliza. "Sorry to cut our visit short, but I only have one hour."

"Go for it. I'll just sit over on the sidelines and do some class prep while I wait for the girls. I haven't ever taught a gardening class before, but apparently that is considered core curriculum in this school."

"It is."

Ava pushed the woman out of her mind and put the class through their paces. If the kids seemed a little careless and wooden today, she'd chalk it up to teacher distraction. How could she work with Eliza watching? Sure, the woman sat with her laptop open, but she still seemed to have plenty of time to keep an eye on Ava.

Could she just let Seth go without a fight?

But she didn't want him. Not really.

Except she did.

And forgiveness was a thing. What was that about his tattoo again? He said it covered up something he didn't want to remember constantly. Did it have something to do with his baby's mother? He was now embracing life. Choosing joy.

She wanted to choose joy. That meant she needed to forgive him, even if he didn't ask for it. He might have tried that day at Main Market Co-op. She hadn't really given him a chance. On the other hand, he knew where she lived. He knew her phone number. He hadn't made a noticeable effort to apologize.

But that wasn't her problem. It was his.

Ava's problem was bitterness. She didn't want to forgive him, even if he groveled. But her relationship with God was suffering. Her relationships with Brittany and Dafne were suffering. And now she was frustrated and angry about Eliza getting the job Ava had hoped for... except she didn't really want it. She wanted another school or two to hire her for music.

Lord? I'll try. I will. But I'm going to need Your strength, because I don't want to forgive Seth. Not for anything.

A man leaned in the doorway of the dance studio, arms crossed. Her heart skipped a beat, but it wasn't Seth. Of course, it wasn't. He'd sent his sisters with their aunt.

But it was her cousin Basil. What was he doing here? In Spokane at all, let alone in the church he'd derided last time she'd been forced to spend time with him?

Ugh. Someone else she held a grudge against. Was God going to make her forgive Basil, too? Please, no.

He looked around the space. Oren, one of Basil's brother Marco's sons, was in Ava's class. But that's not where Basil's gaze lingered for long. Soon he'd focused right in on Eliza sitting along the far wall.

Didn't that just figure? Basil was never one to let an opportunity to flirt with an unattached female pass by, but how could he even tell Eliza wasn't married? Not every woman wore a wedding band.

He sauntered over, and Ava bit back the impulse to scream at him. Or Eliza. Or both of them.

Basil indicated the seat next to Eliza, and she nodded. Then he struck up a conversation. Of course, he did. Had it meant nothing that he'd been watching Hailey like a thirsty man eyed an oasis a couple of months ago?

Basil was insecure.

The realization slammed into Ava. But he couldn't be. Not the guy who thought he was God's gift to all women everywhere, or he'd think that if he was on speaking terms with God.

Focus on class, Ava. Focus.

Somehow, she managed to get through the hour without any major mishaps. The kids weren't at their finest, but neither was their teacher. At least Eliza was too busy lapping up Basil's attention to judge Ava's ability.

That wasn't even funny.

Finally, class ended, and the kids streamed into the foyer. Eliza tucked her laptop into her bag, said a few more words to Basil, waved at Ava, and followed her nieces.

A moment later Ava was left with Basil.

"Good job, cuz. I'm impressed."

"Thanks." She turned away, but her conscience stabbed her. If she was going to start forgiving people who didn't deserve it, maybe she should start with Basil. She glanced over at him. "What brings you back to Bridgeview? It's still a couple of weeks until Tony and Kenna's wedding."

"I'm moving back. Heard there was a vacancy in the Manor."

Seth's apartment, filled again so quickly? "202? That's just below Brittany and me."

"That's the one. Good to know we'll be neighbors in case I need to borrow a cup of sugar."

Ava's eyebrows angled up of their own accord. "So domesticated."

"Hey, I cook. A guy doesn't live on his own for fifteen years without picking up some skills."

"I guess. Are you looking for work?"

"I've been saving up for the past couple of years to buy back into Bridgeview Backyards. I hated making Peter and Jas buy me out to pay off my fines."

She blinked. "Who are you, and what have you done with my cousin Basil?"

"Can't a guy change?"

"You're still making moves on any woman who looks like she might be unattached." Ava indicated the chair Eliza had been sitting in. "That's the same old Basil."

Her cousin chuckled.

Whew. That sounded more like him. Ava wasn't sure she was ready for the axis-shift if Basil turned into a decent guy.

21

*Y*ou can't let your past define you, sis."

Dafne shook her head, "Stop it already." She settled Gavin into a kiddie swing at the playground and gave him a push.

"I'm serious. So, you made a mistake. Haven't we all?" Like Brittany. Ava wouldn't betray her confidence, but there was a case in point, although their cousin wasn't pregnant. For once, the arrival of Britt's shark week had been the source of jubilation in their third-floor apartment.

"Look, I appreciate your support, probably more than you'll ever know. But I didn't just *make a mistake*. I had a baby when I was seventeen. Yeah, Gavin's amazing. I'm not discounting that in the least. But still, I can't rely on some knight in shining armor to swoop in and rescue us both."

They'd reveled in their share of fairy tales as kids, for sure. Princess dreams for the win.

Dafne put up a hand. "Fairy godmothers with magic wands seem to be out of fashion these days. Taking care of Gavin's and my future is up to me."

"Some amazing guy is going to come along. He'll love Gavin as much as he loves you. I just know it."

"You're impossible."

"But I'm right."

"I'm not going to turn him away if he shows up. But I can't make life decisions based on that fantasy."

Ava hated how abruptly her little sister'd had to grow up. "Maybe once you're working, you and I can buy a house together, and I'll keep helping out with Gavin."

"You'll be married long before then." Dafne giggled.

"Not at this rate." But that just brought Seth's kisses to her mind once again. And the chortling baby in his shopping cart, as though he were just some random grocery item Seth had found on the shelves and was purchasing for his sisters.

Yeah, that was enough to douse the longing in Ava's heart.

"What's going on with Seth?"

"Nothing." Ava crossed her arms and turned away. "I've only seen him the one time."

"But the girls are still in dance. Right?"

"Their aunt brings them. The one who got the job I applied for." The one that had bounced into Seth's life just at the same time... wait. Was she the baby's mother? Maybe he wasn't Seth's. Or what if the baby belonged to both of them?

Ava's heart clenched. That couldn't be. Not with the way he'd talked about Eliza and John last month. And Eliza didn't refer to the baby as hers when she brought him to dance.

Leo. The baby had a name. Peyton had announced it.

"You seem far away."

Ava refocused on her sister. "Sorry."

"No problem. Have you been praying about this thing with Seth? I shouldn't even ask. I'm sure you have."

"I was." But then she'd stopped.

"Was?" Dafne's eyebrows rose.

"When I saw the baby, I realized Seth wasn't the man I thought he was. Now my only prayer is to get over him. Move on."

"I thought you were falling in love."

The words were like a stab to Ava's heart. She swallowed hard. "I was." And she hadn't exactly gotten over him, either, no matter how hard she tried. Time. All she needed was more time. Like ten years, maybe.

Dafne gave a gleeful Gavin a push on the swing. "I have a question for you, and I don't want you to be angry. I want you to think about it."

"That's hardly a comforting lead-in." Ava braced herself.

"I couldn't have wished for a better sister than you, ever in my life."

This didn't sound too bad. "Backatcha."

"When I got home from Rob and Bren's and told Mom and Dad I was pregnant, you were there, already defending me."

"Of course. That's what sisters do."

"But I'd messed up big time."

"Well, yeah. But you were sorry. It was totally evident. God forgave you. How could I shun you and wreck the great relationship we'd had all our lives? Besides, you needed me."

Dafne nodded, not looking at Ava as she stopped the swing and lifted Gavin out. He darted over to a low climbing structure.

"Did I miss the question in that?" Ava asked at last. "Because we've been over this hundreds of times."

"And you're always so sure that the right man won't be daunted by my son. He'll love us both and accept Gavin as his own."

"Yes?"

"So... Seth. You have no trouble forgiving me, but what about him? You haven't even given him a chance to talk about that baby. Why do I deserve love and marriage, even though I'm a single parent, but Seth doesn't?"

Ava opened her mouth. Closed it again. Wasn't Seth worthy? Sure, in theory. God had no doubt forgiven him. Ava could forgive him, too, but that didn't mean she needed to get close and set herself up for more pain. She'd known Seth had gone off the deep end for years. That he'd been drinking and partying. Why would she have assumed that didn't mean women? Or was it okay that he'd slept around unless there was a baby to remind her every single minute?

"I just want you to think about it. Pray about it. Because, from over here, it looks like a double standard."

"It's not!" Even to Ava, the protest sounded weak. "There are a lot of differences."

"Sure. But at the core, you think I deserve a chance at a godly marriage, but you don't think Seth does."

"Maybe with someone else."

Only a chance glance revealed the flicker of pain cross Dafne's face. "Come on, Gavin. Time to go."

"No. Wait. Not yet."

"That's all I needed to say, sis. I've got class in an hour and need to get Gav up to Fran's. My classes this semester are kicking my backside."

"You'll do fine. Only two more years, and you'll be done."

Dafne sighed. "Seems forever still. But hey, congrats on landing Southside Elementary! That gives you four schools, right?"

"It does. Big relief. I mean, I'd like five, but four is better than the three I had the past couple of years. And Kass is happy to keep me on Thursday lunch at the bistro."

"I know you like working there, anyway."

"I do, actually. But anyway, I'll pick Gavin up when I get off."

"Thanks, Ava. You're the best." Dafne gave her a fierce squeeze. "You have so much love to give. I'm sure there's enough for a motherless baby in your heart."

Why had she ever told her little sister her dreams of a future with Seth? Why had she admitted she thought she could wrap her brain around caring for his two half-sisters?

Did Seth really deserve not only Ava's forgiveness, but maybe... more?

∽ー᧔ ᧔

SETH STARED AT FRAN. He'd just come by to pick up his son after work — Eliza had taken the girls shopping for school clothes — and the babysitter had ambushed him. "You're kidding, right? There's nothing between Eliza and me. She's my stepmother's sister. That's just... no. No way."

"It's something that crossed my mind, and I thought I'd ask. She's young. Pretty. And devoted to the girls."

Not so devoted to Leo. Shaking his head, Seth looked around Fran's kitchen for the baby. Heartwarming giggles came from the other room. "Eliza's not that young. And there's zero attraction between us." He knew what attraction felt like: Ava. If he didn't like her so much, he might have found humor in her horror at seeing Leo. Or he might have forgotten it by now. Instead, he'd relived the moment numerous times a day for several weeks.

He hadn't found the nerve to track her down and make her listen to his confessions. What good would it do, anyway? None. She was a Santoro of Bridgeview. Any day now, she'd meet some great guy without all this baggage and be relieved to fall in love with him. A guy with a job and a mature faith who didn't have three kids to juggle.

"You care for my cousin, don't you?" Fran asked quietly.

Seth's head jolted, and his eyes met hers. "How did you know?"

Fran offered slight smile. "The grapevine."

Right. He'd known that was a thing. Ignored it. And word of their dance session in Manito Park weeks ago had gotten around. Of course, it had. At the time, he hadn't cared. He'd been cautiously optimistic about the future and thrown caution to the wind for just one evening. All he needed was a decent job, and he could move forward with his declaration of love.

It was more than caring for Ava. He'd gone and fallen in love. He'd tumbled halfway in the night they'd first danced at Alex and Marley's wedding. He'd never wanted anything more than he wanted her... forever.

Seth shook his head, trying to dislodge the melancholy. "It doesn't matter if I do. She doesn't want anything to do with me. Not since she found out about Leo."

"You could possibly have handled that better."

"I'm sure." He hadn't known how, and then it was too late. "But from where things are now, I don't see a way. And the other reasons I should have held back still stand. I'm new to this whole taking-care-of-kids thing. I don't have a permanent job. I don't have my degree. I've got nothing to offer someone like Ava."

Except love, but a girl couldn't live on love. And a family of five definitely needed more.

"Have you been praying about it?"

"Of course." What kind of heathen did Fran think he was?

"Because God has a way of turning things around in ways we least expect. Psalm 37:4." She looked at him expectantly.

"I'm trying to place that."

Gavin ran behind a crawling Leo, herding him toward Seth. He really needed to get the kid home.

"'Take delight in the Lord, and he will give you the desires of your heart.'"

"Aha. I know that one. It means that if you delight in the Lord, your desires will line up with His. It's not a magic wand for getting what you want."

Fran chuckled. "True. But God loves to give good gifts to His children. That's in Matthew seven."

"And again, it's not something I can expect. Ava's her own person. She's decided I'm not a package she wants to receive. She deserves the best, too, and I'm pretty sure I'm not it." Seth lifted Leo into his arms as Gavin scampered off. "I need to get rolling. This guy is ready for dinner, and Eliza and the girls will be home soon."

Fran opened her mouth and closed it again before shaking her head. "Think about what I said. Pray about it."

"Sure." Didn't change anything. He'd been doing both, but the facts stubbornly remained what they were. Seth settled Leo on his hip. "Gotta go." He reached for the door handle just as it swung open.

Ava stopped cold in the doorway, her gaze darting from Seth to Leo then to her cousin. "I'm here for Gavin. I'll be out of your hair in just a minute."

"Ava, wait." Fran took a step forward.

"No, it's fine. Don't let me interrupt. I'm in a hurry." Ava's gaze bounced off Seth again before she scurried through to the other room. "Gavin!"

"Did you do that on purpose, delaying me until she was due for her nephew?"

"Maybe?" Fran had the grace to look chagrined. "But I really did want to say all those things to you. I'm sure God can and will work everything out for your good."

"Yes, I get it. That's in Romans. I promise to keep talking to God, okay?" It's not like it was a faucet he could simply turn off. A few weeks with Leo and without Ava had done little to help him forget her. If anything, he longed for her even more, and it definitely wasn't for the baby's sake.

Ava returned, slinging her nephew to her hip and not meeting Seth's gaze. "Say bye-bye to Auntie Fran, love bug."

"Bye Auntie Fan. Bye Weo." Gavin leaned toward Leo.

Leo clenched and unclenched his fingers in response, a wide grin covering his face. Then he clapped, apparently pleased with himself.

Seth was kind of pleased with the kid, too. And for all Diana's faults — not least of which was keeping him in the dark about Leo's existence — she'd done her best to care for the boy. Now the mantle had been passed, and it was Seth's job to raise him.

Ava's eyes lifted to Seth's for just a second.

This wasn't the shocked, decisive woman who'd fled in

the market. Was she having as much trouble forgetting what they'd shared as he was? But it didn't matter. He had nothing to offer her except three kids... and few funds to raise them with.

"Can we talk?" he blurted out.

It seemed his mouth hadn't gotten the memo, any more than it had that evening in Manito Park. He'd rather spend time kissing Ava again than talking to her, but there were words needing to be uttered. Explanations offered. Hope removed.

"Maybe some time." She grimaced — was that supposed to be a smile? — and grabbed the doorknob. "Bye."

And just like that, she was gone.

22

*H*i, Ava? Can I talk to you for a few minutes?"

Ava turned slowly in the Bridgeview Elementary gym to see Eliza Nelson standing near the bleachers. "Hi. Sure." Not the person she most wanted to talk to, but possibly this had nothing to do with Seth or his sisters. It might have everything to do with teaching, about students they shared and today's music class. This early in the school year, the kids were all excited about learning to play the recorder but were definitely hitting more wrong notes than right ones.

"I heard you'd applied to teach fifth grade here." Eliza took a few steps closer.

Ava forced a smile. "I did, but it's fine, really. I was able to pick up another school for music, which is my preference, anyway. So I'm up to a point-eight position."

"I'm glad it's working out for you. Moving here — getting this classroom — after my divorce has made a huge difference for me, but I hated to think my joy was at someone else's expense."

That word again. All Ava could think of was Seth's tattoo. Was he still celebrating? And, look, there he was with another little life. But it was time for Ava to accept what had happened and put her bitterness behind her. She, too, needed to choose joy, even if she couldn't erase Seth's history or her feelings for him.

Ava took a seat on the bleachers near Eliza. "You know, I'm a Christian. I believe that God has a purpose for my life and that, if I ask Him, He'll guide me. Sometimes that comes across as fatalism to those who don't understand faith, but it really isn't the same thing."

Eliza sat a few feet away and angled herself toward Ava. "I get it. My faith has been weak for a long time, but I've rediscovered it through my divorce and then my move. You're probably familiar with Psalm 18. There's a bit there where David is talking about all the trials he's experienced and then he says about the Lord: 'he brought me into a spacious place; he rescued me because he delighted in me.' That verse has come to mean so much to me lately. I really feel like being able to help raise my nieces is like that spacious place David speaks of."

"That's great." Ava forced a smile. There was no point in telling the woman she felt just the opposite, that the whole situation made Ava feel like she was trapped in a very tiny cupboard.

"Beatrice and Peyton speak so highly of you."

"They're great kids who've been handed a bitter pill."

"They really have, but Seth is so good with them. I tried to talk John into fighting Seth for custody." Eliza took a deep breath and shook her head. "That was before I knew our marriage was on the rocks, obviously. But it's worked out so much better. I'm thrilled I was able to buy a duplex with my share of the proceeds from our Pasco house. It's perfect for us — I live in one half, and Seth and the kids live in the other. We all have our own space, but it makes all the difference for the girls to be able to come and go."

"Sounds lovely." What else was there to say? "I'm glad it worked out for everyone."

"Poor Seth. He didn't even know about Leo's existence until the mother passed away and mutual friends dropped the baby off. I don't know how he manages, to be honest. He has such a big heart — he just takes it all in stride."

Because he chooses life and joy. Enough heart-to-heart. Ava rose to her feet. "I'm glad to hear you're settling in well. Was there anything else? I need to pick my nephew up from daycare, since my sister has classes until five."

"Oh? Where does she teach?"

"She's a student. Two years left in college to become a teacher."

"Good for her!" Eliza stood, grasping her briefcase. "I keep telling Seth not to give up on his dreams of finishing college, but he just doesn't see how right now."

And they were back to Seth... and the things he had in common with Dafne. No wonder Seth had agreed to share Eliza's duplex. Family support meant everything to her sister, too. And Daf had challenged Ava's way of thinking about Seth.

"It's been a rough road for my sister, but she's tough, and she'll make it through." It cost Ava everything to add, "and so will Seth."

Eliza's eyes warmed. It seemed she might have something more to say, but Beatrice and Peyton tore into the gym.

Peyton launched at Ava, squeezing her around the middle. "Hi, Ms. Ava! I miss you."

It wasn't like she'd had a lot to do with the kids, even before, so where was this coming from? "But you see me every week in class and again at dance practice."

"I know, but I still miss you."

Eliza chuckled. "Ready to head home, girls?"

Beatrice crossed her arms but nodded. Peyton gave Ava one more pleading puppy-dog face.

Ava patted the girl's shoulder. "I'll see you tomorrow."

She watched as Eliza and the two children left the gym. Strangely, she felt as though part of her heart walked away with them. She'd once begun to adapt to the thought of the girls in her life, more than a teacher/pupil relationship, but that vision had been ripped from her.

Or had she been the one doing the ripping when she ran away without hearing Seth out? Maybe a little of both.

Little Leo definitely added another layer. Eliza had all but confirmed Ava's suspicion. Leo was Seth's son, but the mother was gone, never to return. Why couldn't she forgive Seth as she had Dafne? Why not extend the same grace to him as she'd given her sister? Why not believe him worthy of respect and love as she believed of Daf?

The clincher was — it was her love on the line. It was *her* life, not some hypothetical person who should forgive unconditionally and love regardless.

She wasn't perfect, either. Just because she hadn't created a child — or managed to avoid it by the skin of her teeth, like Britt — didn't mean she was any better than Seth or Dafne.

Maybe *they* should get together. The two little boys got along great from what she'd seen at Fran's. But as soon as she thought of Seth and Daf as a couple, she rejected the idea.

No. She couldn't give Seth up like that. She had to make a choice: forget him completely or accept him fully. Either way, she needed to forgive him. And that meant hearing him out.

~••~

SETH STARED at the last texts he and Ava had exchanged over six weeks ago now. She'd seemed softer the last few times he'd run into her. She'd sort of agreed to talk sometime, at least in a theoretical sense.

The problem was, he still didn't know what to say. Yeah, things had settled into a sort of routine. Eliza took the girls to school and brought them home. The project for the food forest was complete, but Seth picked up odd jobs here and there. On days he worked, Eliza fixed dinner for them all, but if he was home before her, he did the honors. Either way, Leo was his responsibility. The little guy went to daycare at Fran's as needed.

What could it hurt to text? He needed closure, one way or the other.

Hi, Ava. Still willing to talk sometime? When's good?

He tapped *send* before he could overthink it. Or delete it. Or put it off another week. Then he stared at his phone, waiting for any indication she'd received his message. Or better yet, that she'd respond.

When there wasn't an immediate reply, he stuck the phone in his pocket and crossed the hallway to peek in on Leo. The little guy was sprawled in his crib, the nightlight's glow illuminating his face.

Seth smoothed the hair off the baby's sweaty forehead. Dixie and Dan had given him the crib and a bunch of baby gear since Henry was three now. What would he do without friends like them? Everyone had been so supportive.

Except the only one he cared about. Ava. But he hadn't given her much of a chance. Letting her find out by running into him with a baby had been a cowardly move, and it had backfired completely.

She hadn't texted back yet.

Seth paced into the kitchen. He could eat a house, but they didn't have a lot, and the sensation had to be nerves, not hunger. He passed through into the living room and looked out. Jasmine and Nathan lived across the street. Ava's cousin. He was surrounded, it seemed.

His phone buzzed. His hand dove for the device.

"Seth? What are you doing?" Peyton's sleepy voice came from the loft above.

And this was why Seth couldn't roam the house at all hours. He needed to get a curtain up along the railing, but it hadn't hit the top of his to-do list yet. Or more like, the top of the to-buy list.

"Sorry I disturbed you. Go to sleep, Peyton."

"I can't. Every time I close my eyes, I do my dance routine for Sunday. And then I trip and fall all the way off the stage and break my leg and everyone stares at me while I'm crying. It's terrible, Seth. What if it comes true?"

His phone would have to wait. "C'mere, pumpkin." He sat on the bottom step and patted it.

She made her way down and snuggled against his side.

"Have you ever fallen off the stage?"

She shook her head.

No point in telling her there was almost no chance of

her fears coming true. He couldn't promise. But... "No one would laugh if you fell, honey. They'd come and help you get back up. That's what friends do."

"I don't want to fall. It would hurt."

This from the kid who swung by her knees from the monkey bars? "You've practiced so well. It will all go smoothly."

"But you don't know. You never come to watch anymore."

Her words stabbed him. He'd been leaving anything to do with Bridgeview Bible Church to Eliza. Instead, he'd taken Leo to a church across the city like the scaredy-cat he was. "You're dancing on stage this Sunday? I'll be there."

"Promise?"

"I promise." Even if it meant watching Ava interact with his sisters. Was that text really from her? Or maybe it was Eliza.

Seth pressed a kiss to Peyton's hair. "Go get some sleep. Every time that dream wants to turn bad, you remind yourself that God will take care of you, okay?"

"Okay." She reached over and hugged his neck. "Thanks, Seth. I love you."

"Love you, too. Now scoot. You need sleep before school in the morning."

She scampered up the stairs.

He drew the phone out of his pocket and opened the message app. Not Ava. Disappointment pierced him.

But what was Jacob Riehl texting him for? He barely knew the man. Jacob had invited him to the men's prayer breakfast at the bistro, but between Leo's schedule and not particularly wanting to run into Hailey North, Seth hadn't gone.

You told me you had one year left of an engineering degree... and that you needed a job. Interested in working in a solar engineering office while you finish up part-time? The company I work for, Global Sunbeams, needs an office grunt. Pays pretty decently with room for advancement. Interested?

Seth's heart surged. Would he! His fingers fumbled as he tapped in: *Very much so. Call me? Or send me a link to apply?*

Then he beetled back into his bedroom. No need for the girls to stay awake listening to him talk.

The phone rang with Jacob's name flashing onscreen.

"Hi, Jacob. Thanks for thinking of me. Tell me more?"

"Hey, man. This position has your name written all over it. Global Sunbeams is a great company. I've been here over five years. Early on, I did a lot of international travel with them, but we have a separate team for that now. It was great, but not so nice for family life."

"I'd love the chance to travel someday, but with the responsibility of three kids, this isn't a good time."

"I get that. I've only done a couple of trips since Eden and I were married. Took her on one of them, actually. But with the twins now, I get what you're saying. It's too much to ask her to single parent them for weeks at a time."

Seth forced himself not to laugh. "I've got my stepmother's sister helping with the girls, but that's not quite the same. Single parenting... it's hard. What can I say?"

"Easier with a job, though. A job with options."

"You remember I haven't finished my degree, right? And with three kids, I'm not sure when it could happen." Seth shouldn't have allowed his hopes to climb.

"My boss said they'd pay for your final year if you pledged to stay with the company for... I think he said a decade. You'd need to double-check with him, but it seemed reasonable to me. You'd take your credits over three or four semesters."

Seth sat down on the edge of his bed. "Wait. You already talked to him about me?"

"Yeah? He asked if any of us knew anyone, and the Lord placed you in my mind instantly. I told Dean all about you. He's very interested. When's a good time for his secretary to call you to set up an interview?"

"Anytime tomorrow. Or Friday. Really, I don't have much going on right now."

"Sounds good then. Can't wait to get to know you better as we work together."

"Thanks. You have no idea what this means to me."

Jacob chuckled. "I might have a clue. Talk to you soon."

Seth's phone made two sounds simultaneously. The beep of a call ending, and the buzz of an incoming text.

Ava.

He closed his eyes. *God, thank You. And please keep Your guardian angel hovering near. I still need all the help I can get.*

23

*A*va paced the riverfront walkway near the food forest. Was she crazy? No, she was just hearing Seth out. That put her under no obligation to become a stepmother. There were many steps in between. They could part in half an hour as friends... or, at least, not enemies. Honestly, he probably didn't want any more than that.

She pivoted at the end of the walkway near Myles and Adriana's house and searched the green space as Seth crossed the street from Dan and Dixie's.

Her breath hitched at the sight of him. He wore the gray shorts and striped T-shirt she'd seen many times before, but his hair had been recently cut. It had been getting a little shaggy last time she'd seen him. All the better for her to run her fingers through.

No. She wasn't thinking about that.

Seth angled across the grass toward her. He'd seen her. She wasn't ready. She'd never be ready. *Lord, please...* She didn't even know what to pray.

He stopped a few feet away, his dark eyes taking her in, softening at the sight of her. "Ava."

She managed a smile. "Hey, Seth."

"Want to walk?" He indicated the path she'd trod half a dozen times.

"Okay." This might be easier if she didn't have to look into his eyes. If he didn't have to look into hers, because she'd probably give away her feelings.

"I was fifteen when my mom passed away, seventeen when my dad remarried, and eighteen when Beatrice was born."

Alrighty, then. He was headed for the complete life story. Ava could listen.

"I resented Lori. I felt she trapped my dad into marriage with her pregnancy. I managed to complete two years of college — kind of by the skin of my teeth, to be honest — and then gave up. I could work enough hours here and there to pay for some food and booze. Couch-surfed with friends." He hesitated. "I'm not proud of those years, Ava. I'd been raised in and out of the church. We didn't go all the time, but enough I knew better. I wasn't sure God existed. If He did, He didn't seem relevant. So, I did my own thing. And that included living with a woman named Diana for about six months. Toward the end of that time, I met Dixie. She fascinated me because she knew God was real and was calling out to her, but she was running hard. She made me think."

Ava glanced at Seth as they turned at the east end of the path. He stared off toward the river, his jaw tense.

"I talked to my dad for the first time in several years. And he reminded me of the story of the prodigal son, because he'd recently returned to faith. The story wouldn't let go of me until I turned back to the Father in repentance and accepted His love and His celebration over my return." He chuckled. "I wanted to tell Dixie, but I found out she'd already discovered the story on her own. She'd just become a believer herself."

Ava often sympathized with the older brother in that scenario. The one who wondered why the father would lavish so much on the kid who'd gone his own way while ignoring the kid who'd been faithful.

"I told Diana, but she didn't care. I left. Got a job at a gas station by the freeway and went back to college in the fall. Forged a new relationship with my dad. Learned to appreciate my stepmother. Found I liked my little sisters just fine."

Ava couldn't help smiling. His love of the girls was so evident.

"And then Dad and Lori were killed in that accident in April, and my entire world unraveled. They'd been renovating their house, and it was mortgaged to the hilt. I couldn't afford to keep it. Well, this part of the story you already know." He glanced her way.

She stopped and looked at him. It took a minute for him to actually focus on her without his gaze bouncing off.

Seth reached for her hands but apparently thought better of it, since he then shoved them deep into his pockets. "I had no idea Diana was pregnant. That she'd given birth to my son. That night in June... when you and I had an amazing evening in Manito Park... at least, I thought it was amazing...?"

Ava couldn't have looked away now if she tried. "It was amazing," she whispered.

"I went to Dan's to pick up the girls and found Tanisha

there. She's a friend of Dixie's. A friend of Diana's and mine from the old days. She told me Diana had passed away and that Leo was mine. She handed me a stack of papers, dumped all his stuff into my car, and left."

"That's... harsh."

"I was reeling, Ava. I had no clue what to do. I didn't know how to tell you. How to deal with it at all. I resented him. Resented the girls. Why couldn't I be a normal guy who could court a woman without being encumbered by three kids?"

The anguish in his voice nearly broke Ava. She clenched her arms around her middle to avoid stepping closer and wrapping them around him. He needed comfort. He needed her.

Mostly, he needed to finish his story.

He began to walk again, and she fell into step beside him. "I went to Pasco to see Eliza and John. I was almost certain I was going to let them take the girls, that it would be better for everyone. The girls would have a more stable home, and I could maybe manage one child myself. But then Eliza told me John had just filed for divorce, and her world had come crashing down around her."

What difficult decisions. And his relationship with Ava had been so new, it was no wonder he'd been unable to tell her everything right then.

"Eliza and I hatched a plan where she'd move here if she could find a job. She did, almost immediately. I didn't know at the time that you'd wanted the position. I'm sorry."

"I didn't. Not really. It all worked out."

"Eliza bought a duplex. That's working out well for us to share the girls' care. She helps with Leo a bit, too, but I mostly need help during school hours, so Fran has been watching him some."

"Sounds like you've got everything covered." This was going to be closure, then. Ava managed a smile.

"There's more. I got a job just yesterday. I start on Tuesday, right after Labor Day."

"Nice." Look at him, everything falling into place. Except her.

"It's at Global Sunbeams with Jacob Riehl. I've promised to stay for ten years. In return, they're paying for the final courses for my degree. They'll give me three years to complete everything."

"Wow. That's... above and beyond."

"God. He's amazing." Seth shook his head in wonder. "I can't believe how all this craziness has settled into something so cool. Except for one thing."

Ava's palms grew clammy as Seth turned and faced her from a few feet away.

"It's not fair to you. I had a dream, but so did you. You deserve so much better than a readymade, cobbled-together family. But I can't opt out of raising Leo. He's my child, my responsibility. And I can't opt out of raising my sisters, either. They're finally coming to grips with losing their parents. They've got their aunt, but they need me, too."

Yes, she could see that.

"Ava, you mean a lot to me. This is hard. I need to let you go, but you deserved to hear the whole story. I'm not ending things because I don't care about you. It's the opposite. You deserve so much more than I can ever give." His lips brushed her cheek then he pivoted on his heel and strode away.

Ava's fingers touched her cheek. What had just

happened? Did she have no choice in the matter? He'd decided she couldn't handle his life? That she didn't love him enough?

She could. She did. "Seth?" Her voice croaked on his name. "Don't go."

If he heard, he gave no indication.

"DUDE. She's standing there staring at you with her hand against her face."

Seth pushed past Dan in the doorway without turning to look. "She's still better off without me. Nothing's changed, except now she knows why. She has closure. She can move on now. Find some guy who deserves her, who's not such a hot mess."

Dan closed the door and took Seth's arm, escorting him straight past the kids' toys and out the patio doors. "Sit."

Seth obeyed, dropping his head into his hands.

"Do you believe in redemption or not?"

"I do."

"You're not acting like it."

"Is it wrong to want the best for the woman I love?"

"You are so pathetic." Dan laughed.

Seth's hackles rose. "I know."

"You're missing the point." Dan tapped Seth's tattoo. "What's this again?"

Seth stared at the Celtic symbol. "Embracing life. Choosing joy." But it seemed like he had to choose between them. One meant choosing his son and his sisters. The other seemed selfish. Like he chose Ava but rejected the kids.

"You know what I think you just picked instead?"

Not really. But yes, he did. Seth sighed.

"Bitterness. God has worked out a lot of stuff for you in the past couple of months. Yes, there have been some hard kicks with your parents' deaths, taking on the girls, taking in Leo. But you've had some major blessings, too. Moving to Bridgeview and making friends. Eliza's move, which brought you a place to live and help with the kids. And now this job opportunity at Global Sunbeams."

"You're right. I have much to be thankful for." Too bad the words didn't come with smiley-face sound effects. "I'll get my head wrapped around it all. Promise."

"When did you decide that God's blessings were at an end?"

This time, Seth did look up, sending a scowl at his friend. "What do you mean?"

"What if God wants to bless you with Ava, too? Will you turn Him down because you think you're at quota?"

Was that what he was doing? All those blessings. Could God want to give him one more?

"There's some scripture you need to absorb, my friend. Start with Psalm 30:11 and then follow the thought. I'm gonna go feed the kids some lunch." The patio door slid open then closed, leaving Seth alone on the back deck.

Psalm 30:11? He tapped his way to the reference.

You turned my wailing into dancing; you removed my sackcloth and clothed me with joy.

Huh. That reminded him of a verse from... Jeremiah, wasn't it? He ran a search. There it was. Jeremiah 31:13.

Then young women will dance and be glad, young men and old as well. I will turn their mourning into gladness; I will give them comfort and joy instead of sorrow.

And that led to Isaiah 61.

The Spirit of the Sovereign Lord is on me, because the Lord has anointed me to proclaim good news to the poor. He has sent me to bind up the brokenhearted, to proclaim freedom for the captives and release from darkness for the prisoners, to proclaim the year of the Lord's favor and the day of vengeance of our God, to comfort all who mourn, and provide for those who grieve in Zion — to bestow on them a crown of beauty instead of ashes, the oil of joy instead of mourning, and a garment of praise instead of a spirit of despair.

Sure, those verses were part of longer passages with their own contexts, but when similar words kept reappearing, might it not be considered a more general theme? And if he accepted that, then God might want to give him joy instead of sorrow.

Maybe Dan was right. Maybe he didn't have to walk away from Ava. Maybe there was a way through this together.

Except... he already had walked away, leaving her bereft on the riverbank. And not for the first time.

Seth closed his eyes. In the house behind him, he heard the muted sounds of the children — Dan and Dixie's three and his three. Bless his friends for just stepping in and being God's hands and feet and heart to those who needed help.

He blocked the sounds and reread the passages on his phone. Mulled over the words and what they might mean. Took a deep breath.

And prayed.

24

*D*ixie and Evan were out in the sanctuary, but not Alex. Ava couldn't stall the entire rehearsal, waiting for him to show up. The kids' routines came early in the Sunday school kickoff program. Then, after Pastor Tomas's talk — it wouldn't really be a sermon this time around — the teens would do their routine. Later, she, Dixie, Alex, and Evan would dance to the final song. Alex would be on time. He always was.

She'd rather dance with Seth than one of her cousins, but she had to push him out of her mind. She hadn't seen him since Wednesday by the river.

He was done with her.

Women weren't supposed to chase men, but wasn't that a little old-fashioned for the twenty-first century? Was there any reason she couldn't — shouldn't — text him and tell him she had things to say, too?

Ava Elizabeth! You have sixteen kids staring at you. Lead, already.

Seth had waited this long. He could wait a little longer.

Or possibly a lot longer, since Ava needed to be really, truly sure this was the right way forward. She hadn't even had any real contact with Seth's baby.

"All right, everyone. Line up. Mr. Logan is going to play the piano this time, so it will be a little different than a recording. Mandy, you're first. Then Sebastian. Then Tieri..."

The kids fell into line. They knew their positions, all sixteen of them.

Ava opened the stage door and nodded to Logan Dermott. He grinned and launched into the intro. Even though he'd been the one to record the mp3 they'd been using for practice, the sounds of the actual baby grand reverberating through the sanctuary was fuller. Richer.

This is it.

She nodded to Mandy. The girl might be young, but she was a natural leader as she cartwheeled into position on the far side of the platform.

The others followed, flowing into their eight-minute routine just as they had practiced so many times.

Pastor Tomas offered a thumbs-up at Ava from the front row. A few others sat scattered around the seats. Kass Ferguson watched her stepson, Sebastian, from a seat near the back, with Adriana beside her keeping an eye on Violet. Both women held their toddlers. Near them, Fran and Eliza sat with Leo.

Why did she have the little guy? Where was Seth? Ava frowned for a second. None of her business. *Focus.*

In no time, their part of the dress rehearsal was complete. The kids held their final position until Pastor Tomas mounted the steps and said a few words.

Still no Alex.

Then Ava regrouped them in the ready room. "You guys did great! Were there any surprises? Are you ready for an audience tomorrow morning?"

Manny Ramirez pumped his fist. "So ready!"

Ava laughed. "Okay. Good job. Be here half an hour before the service tomorrow. Your parents know what time, at least if you gave them the information paper last week. Anyone forget?"

The kids shook their head. Peyton looked about to say something, but Beatrice elbowed her. They whispered.

Was this something Ava needed to know? "If you lost the paper, there are a few more copies on the table by the door, so please pick one up on the way out." Did she need to worry about the Donahue girls?

Oh. She nearly clunked herself on the head. She'd said *parents*. The girls didn't have any. Knowing Peyton's literal mind, that was probably it. And Ava needed to be more careful of her wording in the future.

"If your p... pick-up person is here, you may be dismissed. If you want to stay and watch the rest of the program, that's fine, too."

Four teens filed in, ready for their dress rehearsal. Sam Diaz stood in the corner with his eyes shut, mouthing the words to the solo he'd be singing shortly.

Still no Alex.

The teens performed their dance flawlessly. All of them had been in Ava's classes for years and loved to perform.

Pastor Tomas took the platform and said a few words about what he'd say tomorrow.

Sam sang his solo. The kid was good. One of these days he was going to hit puberty, but hopefully not before tomorrow morning.

Dixie and Evan joined her in the ready room. Ava pinned a glare on Evan. "Where's your brother?"

He looked around as though Alex would pop out from behind a curtain any second. "I don't know?"

This wasn't funny. Alex was about the most responsible person Ava knew. He was an *accountant*, for crying out loud. She texted him. *Where are you? Time for dress rehearsal right now!*

It took a few seconds for his reply to come. *Can't make it. Sent a replacement.*

Ava opened her mouth and snapped it shut. No way. This was so unlike Alex. As though some random person could step in at the last second and perform his part.

The ready room door opened, and Ava whirled to face it.

Seth stepped in. "Hi."

"You. What?"

Evan snickered.

Ava glared at him, but he looked wholly unrepentant. Beside Evan, Dixie smirked. They knew. This was planned. Alex hadn't stood her up. Not exactly.

Seth was here. And they were due onstage one minute ago.

He gave her a tentative smile. "Could I have this dance?"

"But..."

"Trust me." He held his hand toward her, palm up.

Maybe he just meant for the rehearsal. Alex would be back for the real thing in the morning. Right?

Logan came back around to their cue, a little louder this time.

Ava could only tell because Dixie had opened the door and stepped out, Evan two paces back. As they'd planned.

There was no time to argue. Seth held her gaze as his chin flicked toward the stage. "Break a leg," he whispered.

She whirled back to the door, only a pace out of sync. She could make that up by the time she found her position.

Could Seth really pull it off? He was a superb dancer with a great sense of rhythm, but this was complex. Well, if not, at least it was only rehearsal. She'd give Alex an earful later.

Ava took her position, poised toward the baby grand.

Logan grinned and nodded as he transitioned into the routine.

She pirouetted... and Seth was right there to swing her to the next position.

"YouTube," he whispered with a grin.

Ava flashed a smile as she spun away toward Evan. Good thing her body knew what to do for the next eight minutes. The choreography was tight, but Seth seemed to be right where he was needed. Any missteps were slight enough no one would notice.

Had he spent the entire night practicing?

For her?

～ℓℓℓ

SETH STOOD on the stage with Ava's hand clasped in his right and Dixie's in his left, with Evan beyond her. They bowed together as the few viewers rose and clapped.

Alex slipped in the door from the foyer and offered Seth a thumbs-up and a grin.

The four of them exited the stage for the ready room. By the time Seth turned to face Ava, Evan had already disappeared into the corridor. Dixie waved as she followed him, a knowing smirk on her face.

"Ava?"

She stopped a few feet away. "How long have you been practicing that?"

"Since last night. Alex showed me, and then I put the YouTube on repeat most of today."

"Why?"

Here went nothing. "Because something occurred to me the other day after we walked along the river."

She waited.

"Life has been filled with so many choices lately. Some of them have been thrust at me, while others have been fairly open. But the choice I wanted most to make seemed too selfish. And, even more, it seemed too selfish to ask of someone else."

"What was that?" Her voice was a whisper.

Seth stepped closer, resisting the urge to reach for her hands. "You. I fell for you when we danced at Alex and Marley's wedding. I've been falling deeper every single day. But there have been so many big things happening, so many obstacles in the way, I knew I couldn't ask you to move forward with me."

"But you didn't give me a choice."

"I know. Dan pointed that out when I left you standing by the river and went back to his place to get the kids. He gave me some verses to read, like Jeremiah 31:13. 'Then young women will dance and be glad, young men and old as well. I will turn their mourning into gladness; I will give them comfort and joy instead of sorrow.'"

"You have a bigger heart than anyone else I know."

Seth swallowed hard as he gazed into her beautiful blue

eyes. "You really think that?"

"I totally do. I could name you dozens of men who wouldn't have met the challenges the way you have. You care about everyone you meet in a way that shames me."

"Shames?" His eyebrows dipped together. "No. What do you mean?"

"For me, it's always been about Ava Santoro. What do I want to do? What would make me happy? What would make me look good? But for you, it's different. You always think of everyone else first. I want to be more like you."

"No, Ava. Don't be like me. Be like Jesus."

"That's what I meant. Because you're following Him in a way I haven't ever had to. My life has been good, and I've made the easy choices that were expected of me, just bobbing along like a branch on the river, taking things for granted."

Somehow his hands clasped hers. He didn't know which of them had reached out first. Maybe it didn't matter, since she gripped back.

"Ava, I don't have the right to ask you this, but would you be willing to give us a try? I know I come with so much baggage. Three kids is a lot to ask of any woman. I don't know—"

Her lips pressed against his.

Against his desires, Seth pulled back. "Are you sure?"

"As sure as I can be today. We've only known each other a few months, but I want to know you a whole lot longer. You asked for a chance. I'll give you that. With all my heart."

"I love you." He'd known it forever, it seemed.

"I think... I think I love you, too."

They didn't need to have all the answers today. Oh, Seth

wanted them. Wanted to move straight from this moment to lifelong promises, but they needed time.

He slipped his hands around her back and pulled her close. "Ava." He put all his longing and hope into her whispered name.

She met his gaze from only a few inches away, her pink lips curving into a smile. "Seth."

And he kissed her, long and deep, his hands caressing her back. He trailed kisses down her cheeks to her exposed neck, her hair conveniently out of the way in a formal bun. He reached for the clip to send the tresses tumbling.

"Ahem."

Seth's hands stilled, but it took a few seconds for his lips to stop moving.

"I see you two have made up."

Pastor Tomas. Seth's face heated as he looked to the pastor standing in the ready room door, a grin on his face.

"Uh, yes." Not that words were needed.

Ava giggled and shifted in Seth's arms to face the door.

"I'd just like everyone together for a few minutes for some final thoughts on what to expect tomorrow before I dismiss you all."

"We'll be right there."

Tomas's eyebrows rose as though he wasn't sure whether he could believe them or not. But the twinkle beneath them belied the sentiment as he pivoted toward the platform.

Seth planted a quick kiss on Ava's mouth, careful not to linger. "Come up to the house for a little while after this? I'll order pizza. I was too nervous to eat before."

Ava looped her arm around his waist as they made their way toward the sanctuary — the long way, where they could slip in the back and be less obvious. "I'd like that."

25

*P*lease, please come in." Mom twisted her apron with both hands as she greeted them at the door after church a few weeks later.

Mom's nervousness had to mean Nonna had arrived first. She stood, unsmiling, in the kitchen doorway beyond.

"Hi, Mom." Ava reached for Leo from Seth's arms, and the little guy came to her readily. They'd spent a lot of time together recently, and she was falling hard. Not just for the baby's daddy, but for the baby himself. "Look what Leo can do!"

She set him on the floor, balancing him for a couple of seconds before letting go. Then he toddled off, only plopping to his diapered bottom when he was halfway across the space.

"Well, isn't he something!" A smile brightened Mom's face.

"He certainly thinks so," Seth said with a chuckle. "Hi, Marietta. You're looking well today."

Nonna actually patted her hair as she smiled at Seth. That guy could charm anyone.

Gavin bounded up the stairs from the basement he shared with his mom.

"Don't forget to latch the gate," Mom admonished, but Gavin had already turned the handle.

"Leo!" he shouted. "Come play."

"Gaga!" Leo crawled to the coffee table and pulled back to his feet.

"It's so cute how he tries to say Gavin's name." Mom looked all teary-eyed as the little guy toddled after the three-year-old.

"He's calling Seth Dada now," Ava said proudly.

Seth chuckled quietly.

Ava's face heated. She wasn't ready to tell anyone Leo was also testing out the word Mama. On her.

"Well, come in. Eliza has the girls today? You know they are all welcome, too. Any time."

"Thanks." Seth gave Mom a side-hug. "She does know, but she wanted to take Beatrice shopping for her birthday, and today seemed the best day to do that. And, of course, Peyton begged to tag along."

"Oh! That girl turns eleven next week, right? We need to make a birthday party for her."

Mom was trying so hard to welcome Seth and the kids into the family. It was like she'd pinned all her grandkid hopes on these three — four, with Gavin. Peter and Sadie didn't seem in any hurry to start a family, but maybe that wasn't a fair observation, since they were still a few weeks shy of their first anniversary.

Nonna lowered herself into an armchair in the living room. "Come, sit with me." She levered a look at Ava.

"I'd love to, Nonna."

Seth dropped a kiss on her cheek. "I'll be in the kitchen helping your mom if you need me."

"Oh, you don't have to!" Mom exclaimed. "Dino will be here in just a minute, and Dafne..."

"That's okay. I want to." He winked at Ava and trailed Mom into the other room.

Ava perched on the edge of the sofa. "Seth's right. You're looking great. It's hard to believe it's been over a year now since your fall."

"I have recovered." Nonna swept her hand to one side as though removing the topic from the list.

"And it's working out well having Tony and Kenna live downstairs?" Their wedding had been a couple of months ago now, and they'd renovated the basement suite to work for them as a couple. That way they were nearby if Nonna needed them, but they weren't in her space every minute.

"Si. They take good care of me."

Right. They'd had this conversation a few weeks ago, too. Ava never knew what to talk to Nonna about. Maybe she should just wait, since it seemed Nonna had a purpose for holding her back.

Patience was hard. Silence was painful.

"So. This Seth. He is a good man, yes?"

"Yes, Nonna. He loves the Lord."

"And those children."

"Yes. Very much. The girls are settling in well. They seem to like Bridgeview Elementary, too, and have made some friends."

"Good, good. And you love him?"

Ava gulped, forcing herself not to glance toward the

kitchen, where she could hear Mom and Seth talking in low tones. "I do. He has made many mistakes, but he—"

Nonna's hand swept the rest of Ava's sentence away. "'For all have sinned and fall short of the glory of God.' And also, 'there is no one righteous, not even one.' This is why we need a Savior."

Ava blinked back tears.

"'For the wages of sin is death, but the gift of God is eternal life in Christ Jesus our Lord.'"

Why had she forgotten what a fountain of wisdom and biblical knowledge her grandmother was? Why had she assumed Nonna would judge her or Seth and find them wanting? "Yes," Ava whispered. "Jesus' gift of salvation extends to all who believe. Seth believes, and so do I."

Her grandmother nodded. "This brings peace and joy. It does not mean there won't be hard times. Then we cling to our Savior even more, and He will see us through. Do you know this?"

"I do. I once looked for Mr. Perfect, forgetting there is no such thing, but that believers are clothed in Jesus' righteousness and forgiveness. If He wipes away all guilt, who am I to remember it?" Seth might not be Mr. Perfect, but he sure seemed like her own perfect match.

"As Second Corinthians 5:17 says, 'Therefore, if anyone is in Christ, the new creation has come: The old has gone, the new is here!'"

"Exactly."

Nonna patted Ava's hand. "It is good to see you growing in your faith. To see you falling in love with a good man who loves the Lord."

"I have so much to be thankful for. God has been so good to me."

"My beloved Italia was torn by war when I was a small child. My mama and papa brought us to the United States for new opportunities. So, God's goodness — this I understand."

Why had Ava never asked for stories of Nonna's childhood? She knew a smattering of facts, but she'd never spent as much time with Nonna as some of her cousins had, like Jasmine. Nonna always scared her a little. Maybe it was because Mom always seemed nervous around her mother-in-law, but then, Mom was nervous about many things. Huh.

Ava gave Nonna a hug around the shoulders. "I love you, Nonna."

Tears sprang to Nonna's eyes. "And I love you, my child. Family is a good thing, yes?"

"It is. Thanks for everything."

"Ava?" Mom's voice came from the doorway. "Can I get you to give me a hand, or am I interrupting something?"

"I'm coming."

⁂

SUNDAY LUNCH AT AVA'S PARENTS' house had gone well, but Seth was always happy to leave since her grandmother's presence seemed to make Ava uptight. Today seemed different.

They'd gone back over to the duplex, where Seth tucked Leo in for his nap while Ava folded baby clothes from the dryer. Then they poured a couple of coffees and went out to the backyard to catch the gorgeous fall afternoon. Eliza and the girls would be back soon, but they had a few minutes to themselves. Hopefully.

Seth tucked Ava against him on the patio swing. "You seem more relaxed today." He hated mentioning it in case it was his imagination.

"I realized something about my nonna."

"Hmm?" He started the swing with his foot and rested his cheek on her hair. Thankfully she wasn't wearing a bun today. Those were full of stabby things.

"She's blunt. She can be harsh. But she loves her family deeply, and her God even more."

"Umhmm?" Seth could have told Ava all that.

"I want to be just like her when I grow up."

Seth chuckled, his hand smoothing the sleeve of Ava's turtleneck. "You seem pretty grown-up to me. And you already have all her best qualities."

"This must be why I appreciate you so much. You know all the right things to say."

He shifted slightly so his other hand could cup her cheek. "Only appreciate? I was thinking something more. Something deeper, more lasting."

She smiled against his palm but didn't look up.

"How about love? Because I love you, Ava Elizabeth."

"I love you, too. And I don't even know your middle name. There's lots I don't know, but I know you're amazing."

"Flatterer. My middle name is Jonathan."

"Seth Jonathan Donahue," Ava said softly. "I love you."

Peace flooded Seth's heart. Could anything be more precious than mutual love between a man and a woman, both bent on loving God first? This was still all so new, so sweet, but it had been tested by fire.

Patience, Seth. Give this love time to mature.

He didn't want to, but he knew to follow this prompting

in his spirit. Someday, Lord willing, he'd ask Ava to marry him, but not today. Not yet. He needed to finish melding his life with Beatrice and Peyton and Leo before he could give Ava all the attention she deserved. He needed to settle into his new job at Global Sunbeams, which he'd loved from the first day.

"Soon, Ava, my love," he whispered into her hair as he tipped her face toward him.

"What is soon?" Her blue eyes gazed into his.

He kissed her nose. "I'll tell you... soon."

"Sounds like quite a tease."

"Then how about this?" And he kissed her thoroughly until both of them were breathless.

*A*utumn edged into winter as leaves fell and winds blew. Snow blanketed the city, and they celebrated with sledding and ice-skating parties followed by long cozy evenings of games, hot chocolate, and popcorn around the fireplace.

Ava loved having two weeks off teaching over Christmas break. She and Eliza painted and danced with the kids while Seth worked and studied. They spent Christmas Day with Ava's family, and her parents showered gifts on the two little boys and the two big girls.

Leo called her Mama.

Ava's heart was full. Full of love, but also full of expectation.

And now fragrant blossoms erupted on fruit trees all over Bridgeview. Songbirds trilled and made nests in the blush of spring.

Spur of the moment, Eliza offered to take Leo to the park with her and the girls one evening, and Seth turned to Ava with brightness shining in his eyes. "We can't let this opportunity go to waste! Have you been by the food forest lately? I want to see how it looks."

She didn't need a second invitation. "Let's go." She kissed Leo's plump cheek and handed him off to Eliza.

Seth took her hand, and they headed down the hillside toward the river. Ava would worry about the return climb later. They didn't get a lot of time alone.

"It's looking good. I should start picking rhubarb again soon."

"But you're not working at the bistro anymore."

She chuckled. "You and the kids and teaching keep me too busy."

He turned toward her and looped his hands around her waist. "Do you miss it?"

"Not really. I'm thankful for the time I spent there. It was a fun job while I needed it."

Seth searched her eyes. "I'm thankful for the few times I worked for Hailey, too. If I hadn't served at Alex and Marley's wedding, when would we have met?"

"A few weeks later, right here, over the rhubarb patch. I remember the day." Ava tugged his hand away from her hip so she could trace his tattoo. "Celebrate life. Choose joy."

"Will you choose me?"

Before she realized what he was doing, Seth dropped to one knee right there beside the row of junipers, holding out a tiny velvet box.

She'd known this was coming. Of course, she'd known, and she'd been patient. But she still couldn't hold back the gasp at the sight of the princess-cut diamond glistening in its satin nest. "Oh, Seth! It's beautiful."

"Will you marry me, Ava Elizabeth? I love you more

than I could ever tell you, but I plan to try, every day for the rest of our lives."

"I love you, too." She tugged him to his feet and wrapped her arms around his neck. "I'd like nothing better than to marry you."

"I'm a package deal," he said with a warning chuckle between kisses.

"Don't I know it? But you're a package I'm delighted to accept. You and Leo and Beatrice and Peyton."

"Eliza said she'd keep all the kids when we go on our honeymoon."

"She knew?" Ava tilted back her head to look in Seth's eyes. "That's why she took them tonight?"

He nodded then rested his forehead against hers. "I know it's a strange setup..."

Ava stretched and kissed him. "I've known that for a long time, and it hasn't scared me away yet. Put that ring on me, Seth Jonathan Donahue, and let's decide when."

It took a few minutes for him to stop kissing her in return, but he finally slid the ring onto her finger. She rested her hand on his shoulder to admire the way it caught the evening sun. "It's beautiful, Seth. I love you."

He clasped her hand with one of his and rested the other on her waist, giving her a little twirl. "Could I have this dance for the rest of my life?"

Strains of Anne Murray's classic song played through Ava's mind as Seth led her through the steps as they'd done when they first met, a year ago. He heard the music as fully as she did, as though their hearts were already one.

And both their hearts chose joy.

DEAR READER...

Thanks for reading *Joys of Juniper*! I'm so honored that you chose to spend the last few hours with Ava, Seth, and me. You are appreciated.

I'm an independent author who relies on my readers to help spread the word about stories you enjoy. Would you take a few minutes to let your friends know? Facebook, Instagram, Goodreads... wherever you hang out online.

Also, each honest review at online retailers means a lot to me and helps other readers know if this is a book they might enjoy. I'd sure appreciate your help getting word out.

I welcome contact from readers. At my website, you can contact me via email, read my blog, and find me on social media. You can also sign up for my newsletter to be notified of new releases, contests, special deals, and more! You'll receive *Promise of Peppermint*, the ebook novella that introduces Bridgeview — Rebekah and Wade's story — absolutely free as my thank you gift!

Keep reading for a sneak peek of the next Urban Farm

Fresh Romance book, *Together in Thyme* (Hailey and Basil's story). Enjoy!

~ Valerie Comer

www.valeriecomer.com

http://valeriecomer.com/subscribe

Together in Thyme

USA Today
Bestselling Author

VALERIE
COMER

CHAPTER 1

Together in Thyme
An Urban Farm Fresh Romance 12

*H*e was back in town.

Hailey North hated that her heart sped up at the thought. She'd been doing just fine without Basil Santoro in her life, thank you very much. Three years since he'd left Bridgeview in disgrace. Over one thousand days she couldn't decide if she wished he'd return or stay away forever.

Fickle heart.

She should hate him.

She kind of did. And there was no way she was fixing the guy a coffee or even talking to him, if she could help it, even if he'd come into her public place of business. "Astrid! You're needed over here."

The middle-aged server glanced over. "Coming right up." She patted a woman's shoulder as she topped off her coffee cup.

Basil shifted closer to the counter. "What, you don't know how to use your own fancy coffee machine?" Amusement glinted in his blue eyes.

"I run the kitchen. Kass runs the floor." Only, her cousin's toddler had thrown up all night, and Kass had begged off. They usually had enough staff to cover, but Bridgeview Bakery and Bistro had been busier than usual all morning, and Hailey had been called out of the kitchen more than once.

"What can I get you?" Astrid asked Basil.

Basil's eyes lingered on Hailey, but she turned away. She could answer the question for him, unless working at the Fireweed in Seattle had fancied him up. For Basil, it had always been...

"Just coffee. Black."

And he hadn't changed. He was likely incapable of it. Something she needed to do a better job of keeping in mind.

"Do you have a few minutes, Hailey? You look like you could use a break."

Why couldn't he leave well enough alone? She stilled in the doorway to the kitchen. Such flattery, telling a woman she looked tired. "Sorry. Too much to do." Too many things to forget.

"It is your usual time for a break. There's been a bit of a lull, and Julissa comes in in five minutes."

Thanks, Astrid. "I'd rather n—"

"You're afraid of me, Hailey? Tsk."

She pivoted back and gave Basil a hard glare. "Afraid of you? Not in your wildest dreams."

His eyebrows bobbed as a grin creased his face. "Oh, I wouldn't want to tell you about my wildest dreams. Or... maybe I should?"

Hailey stiffened. If she could throw the guy out into the busy street on his backside, she'd do it in a heartbeat. After all the things he'd done to her. Things no one knew, but he sure did. Well, he didn't know everything, and she wasn't going to enlighten him.

This was her place of business. Hers and her cousin's. She couldn't yell and scream and demand he leave the premises, but it would certainly be therapeutic.

Not that he'd listen. That sardonic grin was his trademark. The only time she'd seen it disappear was when he'd been sentenced to jail after his drunk driving conviction three years ago. The facade had shifted then. He'd done his time then moved to Seattle, but it didn't look like he'd transformed at the core.

Rumor had it he'd stopped drinking, not that Hailey paid attention to gossip. Okay, she totally did, especially if Basil's name came up. And if the source was one of Hailey's closest friends, Basil's sister, Jasmine. That pair of siblings had never gotten along as kids or even as adults, and Jasmine had been furious with Basil over that episode. Not only for driving under the influence, but because he had Dixie in the car with him. Dixie, who'd been living with someone else.

Hailey shoved all that out of her head.

Astrid rang up Basil's coffee.

He raised his eyebrows at Hailey. "Come on, Hailey. I don't bite."

Not exactly how she remembered him.

Basil smirked.

"A hazelnut latte, Hailey?" asked Astrid. "I can fix it with monk-fruit sweetener and even go decaf if you prefer."

"Sugar-free. Impressive." Basil took a sip from his mug, his gaze still fixed on Hailey.

"We try to flex with the times." Hailey stared him down. "Lots of folks are trying to cut sugar out of their diet, and they bring us a brisk business."

"Please don't tell me you've tampered with your cinnamon roll recipe."

"Never."

Astrid coughed.

Hailey sighed. "We did introduce a keto version as well, but it's not been as well-received." Astrid had poked and harassed Hailey and Kass to expand into that market, and it had been worth it. Now Astrid acted like she was part-owner instead of part-time staff. That she was a shirt-tail relative of Kass's didn't help the woman's attitude.

Basil pulled his wallet back out. "Well, now you have me curious. I'd like to try the keto version."

Hailey narrowed her gaze at him. "It's on the house." Why on earth had she said that?

His eyebrows shot up.

Maybe she'd done it to shock him, and it had worked. She picked up the tongs, set a roll on a small plate, and handed it across the turquoise bakery case. "I'll be interested in your thoughts."

No, she wouldn't be.

"I'm happy to pay..." He studied her face. "Never mind. Thank you."

The espresso machine hissed, but Hailey didn't break

her gaze from Basil's. It might be childish, like whoever looked away first was the loser. Or she might just be filling her memory banks with his blue eyes, his curly dark hair, the scruff on his chin.

"Join me?" he asked again, quieter.

"Here's your hazelnut latte, Hailey." Astrid set it on the counter. "Sugar-free."

Now she'd look like a petulant child by rejecting, but she'd speak to Astrid later about usurping authority. "Fine. I can take five minutes."

"Julissa can finish up lunch prep when she comes in," Astrid said.

That woman. Why couldn't Hailey fire Astrid again? Right. She was Kass's husband's ex-mother-in-law. That *ex* should count for something.

"Preference where we sit?" Basil poked toward the corner table with his chin.

Hailey was going to regret this big time. She already did... except for the part of her that thrilled to his nearness.

She wouldn't think twice about sitting down with any of their other male clients, including Basil's brothers or cousins. She'd only flirt with the singles, of course.

But Basil? He'd always been in a category of his own. Like playing with fire.

She'd already been burned.

⁂

BASIL SANTORO WOULD TOTALLY HAVE GONE for the fist-pump if he didn't have a plate in one hand and a mug in the other. Of course, the action would have backfired. Hailey would hightail it back into the bistro's kitchen quickly enough to create a hurricane-force wind, but seeing her angry was kind of a win on its own.

Yeah, yeah. Not a grownup thought and, at thirty-three, he should be well on his way to adulthood. Wasn't that everyone's comment to him all the time? *Grow up, Basil.* This time he heard it in his sister Jasmine's voice.

He settled into the bright yellow chair in the corner and glanced toward the counter. Yep, this spot still had a perfect view straight into the depths of the cooking area. It might not be fair to make Hailey sit with her back to her customers, but whatever. He'd be here long after she stormed off in anger or frustration.

Basil broke off a piece of the cinnamon roll and glanced at Hailey.

She'd only improved with age, much like a fine wine. Right, he wasn't thinking about alcohol these days. She must be thirty now — she was his sister's age, and Jasmine had turned the big three-oh in spring. Hailey wore her blond hair chin-length, and while she wore a bouffant cap in the kitchen, she'd shed it at the kitchen door.

Vain, his Hailey.

Only... not his.

"Looks like you guys keep busy. You've been open, what, six years now?"

She nodded. Sipped her latte.

What must it be like to have a vision for one's future, buckle in through thick and thin, and make a go of it?

Basil had drifted. He'd tried the college thing, but dropped out and drifted from one job to the next. His older brother, Marco, had helped him get a job with City of Spokane Public Works. He'd done everything from shoveling sidewalks to fixing manhole covers and watering flower boxes. Whee. Talk about fulfilling.

"You afraid of a keto cinnamon roll?" Hailey eyed the pastry still in his hand.

"Should I be?" He quirked an eyebrow at her as he popped the bite into his mouth. The temptation to dramatize gagging then holler for water flared, but he withstood. "Not bad. The texture isn't as melt-in-your-mouth as the originals, though."

Hailey visibly relaxed. "Almond flour just doesn't react the same as wheat."

Huh. She actually cared about his opinion? "No, it doesn't."

She looked at him, eyebrows raised. "You've been experimenting?"

"You have no idea what I've been doing the past few years."

"Serving at a restaurant in Seattle."

Basil grinned. "The most highly reviewed upscale restaurant. Tips were amazing."

"Well, that's nice for you, I'm sure. Thanks for gracing my humble establishment, which is nothing as fancy as what you're accustomed to."

Ooh, those blue eyes shot daggers at him. This was more the Hailey he knew and loved. No. Not loved. He'd burned any potential bridges a long time ago now. "This place has plenty of hometown charm."

"Just call it quaint and be done with it."

"Okay. Quaint."

"Some things never change." She gritted her teeth.

"You told me to say that." He leaned across the table and looked her in the eye. "I always do what you tell me."

Red flashed up her cheeks, and she surged to her feet. "You're insufferable."

"As you say." For a second, she looked like she'd dump the remains of her latte in his lap, but she swept away. Behind the counter, she emptied her mug down the drain then set it in the bin before grabbing her hairnet and entering the kitchen.

"What's with Hailey?"

Basil looked up to see his cousin Peter setting his briefcase on the vacated chair. He shrugged. "You know how she gets in these moods."

Peter frowned thoughtfully. "I'm going to grab a coffee. Be right back. Hey, is that one of the keto cinnamon rolls? Sadie loves those things."

"Yeah. Not bad."

"Not bad? Hailey is a genius with recipes."

Thankfully, Peter didn't wait for a reply but headed for the counter. The short woman — Astrid, Hailey had called her — rang up his order then Peter returned and removed a sheaf of papers from his briefcase.

"You sure you want to do this?" Peter studied Basil.

Time for that grownup bit to kick in. "Absolutely. I've been socking away as much as possible for three years. I'm ready to buy back in."

"Things are different now. Your sister and I have worked our fingers to the bone to get Bridgeview Backyards where it is now. We're farming fourteen backyards and have dozens of subscribers to the organic box program. And we're always scrambling for seasonal workers. Jason and Landon both graduated from high school in May and are headed away for college soon. We can't count on them coming back next summer... and we still have a brutally busy wrap-up in the next couple of months."

"How does Jasmine manage with a toddler?"

Peter looked at him as though Basil should know the answer already. "Lillian is in daycare in the mornings, and then Nathan keeps her for the afternoon. Thankfully, he works from home and can manage his clients while Lillian naps."

Jasmine was nothing if not dedicated. Basil had to hand it to her. She would have been the perfect firstborn in their family but had landed in the middle with two brothers in front and two behind.

Astrid set Peter's coffee down and topped off Basil's without asking if he wanted more. When she moved on to the next table, Peter handed the papers over to Basil. "I want you to take your time and read through all of these before committing. This is our updated business plan and our financial statements."

Did Peter need to sound like he thought Basil would bail out on them again? As though he'd enjoyed leaving the company in a lurch three years ago! No one wanted to be hauled through court and force his partners to buy him out to pay his fines. Yeah, he'd pretended it was no big deal. What else was he supposed to do? Apologize? Grovel? That wasn't his style.

Maybe it was time for a different way.

Movement in the kitchen caught Basil's eye. Hailey leaned over her work table, rolling out pastry. She looked strong. In control.

Gorgeous.

Wasn't stupidity doing the same thing over and over but hoping for different results?

Actually, changing meant admitting he'd been wrong all these years. That he'd been selfish. Arrogant. Everyone who knew him already knew all that.

But maybe it meant letting his guard down. Letting people see who he was on the inside. They wouldn't like him any better with the added insight.

Especially not Hailey.

ABOUT VALERIE COMER

Valerie Comer's life on a small farm in western Canada provides the seed for stories of contemporary Christian romance. Like many of her characters, Valerie grows much of her own food and is active in the local foods movement as well as her church. She only hopes her imaginary friends enjoy their happily-ever-afters as much as she does hers, shared with her husband, adult kids, and adorable grand-daughters.

Valerie is a *USA Today* bestselling author and a two-time Word Award winner. She writes engaging characters, strong communities, and deep faith into her green clean romances.

To find out more, visit her website at www.valeriecomer.com, where you can read her blog, explore her many links, and sign up for her email newsletter, where you will find news, giveaways, deals, book recommendations and more. You can also find Valerie blogging with other authors of Christian contemporary romance at Inspy Romance.

www.ingramcontent.com/pod-product-compliance
Lightning Source LLC
Chambersburg PA
CBHW050723180626
46814CB00002B/580